LOVE HEIST:

HE ROBBED MY HEART

A Novella

By

Ms. Grad Marie

Quote

"When there's a single thief it's robbery, when there are a thousand thieves it's taxation."

- Vanya Cohen

Synopsis

Gwop, Darren Thompson, is the co-leader of one of the most notorious, but anonymous robbery gangs in the United States of America, "Stack Gang". His job is to case out each location before his crew robs them blind, leaving no witnesses behind. During the scope of his crew's next big heist, he is enticed by Shiri Marks, whose southern beauty causes him to fall off his game a bit.

Shiri is a naïve, still-wet-behind-the-ears daddy's girl who is new to the tri-state area. She came to begin a new life and pursue her career, finally cutting the umbilical cord from her overbearing parents back home. She soon meets a kind, but rough-around-the-edges gentleman, who introduces her to the East Coast lifestyle.

Little does Shiri know; her prince charming has ulterior motives. She finds out the truth about his career during a very awkward moment. She felt her new man had robbed her heart in a good way, but she ends up a hostage in his sticky situation.

Gwop is torn between who he really is and who he's trying to be. The number one rule of this crew is to never let your true identity be revealed. If so, you can't leave any witnesses behind. When Shiri finds out the truth about her true love, will she be willing to risk everything she's worked hard for? Or will Gwop dishonor his brother by giving up on the family business to be with the love of his life?

♥PROLOGUE♥

GWOP

You might win some, but you just lost one

You might win some, but you really lost one

You just lost one, it's so silly how come?

When it's all done, did you really gain from

"Lost Ones" by Lauryn Hill played loudly through the speakers as Sweetie put her stiletto to the medal and headed towards the freeway. I shook my head and thought, can this bitch do a job without music?

"Sweetie!" I yelled to our getaway driver. "Go, go, go!" I loaded my AK-47 and cracked open the van's back window and lit up the scene with my ammo, making that bitch look like it was the Fourth of July.

Pow! Pow!

The armored truck officer bust his gun towards us, shattering the back window as Sweetie skidded on the loose gravel down the dark alley.

"Mikey! Mikey!" I called to my partner, who was laid out on the van's floor, suffering from gunshot wounds to his thigh. We hadn't realized he had been hit until after he hopped in the van after snatching two sacks of crispy Benjamin Franklins from the money truck guard earlier, during one of our many planned robberies.

"Mikey, answer me!" I yelled again, reloading my gun to aim back at my target, the armored trucks driver.

Pow!

One shot from my rifle to his head and he was instantly executed. I smiled sinisterly as he and his truck fell over the shoulder of the freeway and into the

Mississippi River. I felt a great deal of achievement, knowing my big brother would be proud.

I pressed my back against the inside of the van, breathing heavily. I soon snapped back to reality as I looked over at Mikey. I placed my gun to the left of me and crawled over to him.

"Come on, bruh, come on. Answer me, please!" I shook his body as his eyes stared back at me with no motion or life in them. I put two fingers to his neck and checked his pulse. Thank God, he was still breathing.

"Sweetie!" I called to her again as she drove frantically, praying in Spanish for our friend's life. "Get us to the safe house, now! Call Bang and tell him to get Dr. Easy on the way, stat! He's not responding and has already lost too much blood."

"Yes, brother. I'm calling him now, Gwop. Stay up, Mikey, stay up! Don't you close your eyes on us, Papi. Señor, por favor, salve a Mikey. Señor, por favor, salve a Mikey." She cried to Jesus, begging Him to save Mikey's life in her language while she made the phone call to my brother. I pulled our wounded soldier in my arms tightly and rocked, praying for him myself.

Mikey was only nineteen years old. He was too young to lose a life he had yet to begin living. I'd previously told my older brother, Bang, our little partners, Pilla and Mikey, were too young to join our robbery squad, but he didn't give a fuck. The only nigga he gave a damn about was Benjamin Franklin and the other dead presidents.

Even though we were the most anonymous and notorious robbery gang, this shit was starting to get old to me. We were born and raised in the tri-state area, but we had never done a job in or near our hometown of Elizabeth, New Jersey. It was too risky. We'd traveled around the world to many states to fulfill our greed and had never been caught. We never hit the same city or state more than once. The reason why was because we never left a paper trail or any witnesses.

I'd killed many niggas in my profession, but I had a double standard when it came to members of my group, my own family. Honestly, I didn't feel that any amount of money was worth taking a life over.

"We have to switch cars now, Gwop!" Sweetie yelled from the driver's seat as she zoomed into a dimly lit parking garage, breaking the entrance gate on her way in.

She parked next to a black Nissan Sentra and hopped out to hotwire it.

I let go of Mikey and leaned back on my knees, opening the back door. I placed both hands on my face and shook my head in distress.

"The car is ready. Come on, Papi," Sweetie said as she pulled Mikey's lifeless legs to help him out the van.

"His eyes closed, ma, he's gone!" I cried as I fell to the ground, staring at his body.

"No, please no!" Her screams echoed through the vacant car parking garage as her medium-brown mascara ran down her pretty face.

BANG

"What, Sweetie? Calm down for me, babe. I can't
understand that Spanglish you speaking right now, shorty."
I pulled over to the corner of Canal Street.

"It's Mikey, love. He—" I removed my ear from the
phone as I scanned my rearview mirror and saw two
detectives walking up behind me. I threw my car in drive
and sped through the downtown streets of New Orleans as
another squad car followed closely on my tail. My
adrenaline rose with each turn I made in hopes of fleeing
the cop cars that were following closely behind me.

"Fuck!" I screamed as I realized my cell had hit the
floor panel. I reached down to retrieve it as my car swerved
into oncoming traffic. I darted down a dark alley and
decided to do the unthinkable when I saw the cops were no
longer that close behind me, but I could hear their sirens
approaching my location. I secured my M 11911 .45
Caliber Ghost Gun in my pants, grabbed my phone from
the floorboard, and turned off my car lights. I opened my

door and jumped out of my moving car, rolling onto the gravel of the dark alley, hiding my body from any potential witnesses. I heard a loud crash and saw that my car had slammed into a city bus and another small vehicle.

Fuck, fuck, fuck! I thought as I jumped to my feet and ran down the alley like Carl Lewis looking for a getaway. Being that I had on all-black during the robbery, I decided to shed some of my clothes to easily blend in with the crowd of drunk partygoers who were partying in the street. I pulled my black hoodie over my head and tossed it inside a makeshift heater some homeless bums nearby had made with an old trashcan. I pulled a stack of money from my pocket and gave both homeless women a crispy hundred-dollar bill.

"See, Bennie, I told you there are still some good people in this crazy world. Let's go down and get us some wine to celebrate. Thanks, Hun." I waved to them and smiled as I turned the corner from the alley to blend in with the crowd and placed my cell to my ear, waiting for my Sweetie to answer.

"Aaron Thompson! Put your hands up! We've got you. It's been a long journey, but now it's time to surrender! Your days of stealing from the government are finished. You're mine now, nigga!" Detective Marissa Benson shouted in my ear as she pulled my hands down from the air and placed them behind my back to cuff them.

Of all the years my crew had robbed people, we'd always gotten away. I admit I was cocky because we'd never been caught, but this time, we had gotten caught slipping. "Oh, I see you are very excited to see me." She smiled sarcastically as she looked down at my hard dick. I always had an instant erection after a successful getaway. I fucked Sweetie from time to time, but money was what really made me cum.

I sucked my teeth at her as my penis softened. My blood boiled inside. There was no way I would spend one fucking day in prison, and I meant that shit.

Present Day

♥Chapter One

SHIRI

"I'm going to miss you so much, love bug," my mother, Tasha, said as she squeezed me in her embrace.

"Now, baby girl, remember to not look up high when you're walking, keep your eyes straight ahead, but still keep a 360-degree awareness at all times. Don't look as if you're sightseeing because muggers can quickly tell you are not from the area," my father, Brandon, reminded me as he lifted my luggage out the trunk of his BMW.

"Yes, daddy. I'll remember everything, and Khodi said she will be picking me up from the airport as soon as my plane arrives," I told him.

"Ugh, baby girl, I'm really going to miss you." My mother cried as she grabbed my hands and pulled me into a tight embrace. "Since you're leaving, who am I going to spend my Saturday mornings with, getting my weekly treatments at the spa?"

"Mommy, I'm not leaving forever. I promise to come visit as soon as I can." She hugged me again, and I rolled my eyes behind her back. "I have to go now; check-in starts in ten minutes."

I extended the handle on my suitcase and waved again before walking to the entrance doors of the airport, ready for my flight, then halted and turned to look at my parents again. "Oh, yeah, be sure to tell BJ I said good luck at his chess competition tomorrow. I'll talk to him as soon as I land. I love you all." I blew a kiss to my parents and hurriedly walked into the airport, disappearing amongst the busy crowd to find the check-in station.

Even though the airport was extremely busy, I was super excited about beginning my new life, far away from my controlling parents. It was beyond time. I was now a twenty-three-year-old grown woman with an MBA in accounting, and I still lived at home with my parents.

My father, Brandon Marks, was a prominent attorney of his self-owned law firm in Atlanta, Georgia, where we were from. My sixteen-year-old brother, Brandon Jr., and I went to the top-rated private schools growing up. We were both in the top three percentiles of our classes.

We grew up in a well-balanced, two-parent, good Christian home, and our parents were very involved in our lives, and we had no privacy. My parents strongly believed their children should live under their roof until we were mentally equipped to face adulthood alone.

After graduating from Georgia State University last year, I worked at a local, family-owned credit union as an accountant for one of our church members, Deacon Collins. Sadly, he passed just six months ago, and the family decided to close the business due to the revenue decreasing since his death. My father told me I could stay at home and go back to school for my minor, business administration, but I decided against it. I was saved by the bell when my best friend and play cousin, Khodisha, called me, letting me know her branch had an opening for an accountant with the degree I had worked so hard to achieve.

We had been best friends since grade school, we lived in the same neighborhood, and our fathers were partners of their joint law firm, Attorneys of Marks & Roberts. My parents were doubtful at first of their oldest and only baby girl traveling 2,500 miles across the states to take on a career up north in Berkeley, New Jersey, but I was more than ready. It was time I start my journey in adulthood. I must admit, I was indeed nervous because I'd never been this far away from my parents before. I was ready to come out for the interview process, but because of the distance of my residence, the branch decided to do my hiring process via webcam. Khodi was the assistant supervisor of Tri-State Financial, so that helped my parents approve of me accepting the faraway job.

My parents and I took family trips yearly, so this wasn't my first time on an airplane, but it was my first time I would be flying alone.

I sat in the waiting section of the loading area and scrolled my Instagram newsfeed. My parents didn't approve of us having social media pages, so I'd made one under a fake name.

RING! RING!

"Yes, dad?" I exhaled and rolled my eyes as I answered my cell.

"Just wanted to tell you I love you, baby girl, and to please call as soon as you get settled in. Now, you remember everything I told you. And know that if you ever feel like you want to leave and come back home, Daddy will come get you."

"We love you, baby girl!" I heard my mother sob into the phone receiver.

"South Delta Airlines is now processing on boarders, now processing on boarders. One-way trip to Newark, New Jersey, to Newark Liberty International Airport. Boarding now."

The speaker sounded above my head, letting passengers know it was now time for boarding.

"I love y'all, too, daddy. And don't forget to kiss BJ for me. They're calling for my section to board now. I'll call you when I make it."

"Sure thing. Safe travels, Daddy's princess." I smiled as we ended the call. I grabbed my white, floral, Betsey Johnson carry-on bag as I walked over to the boarding line.

"Hi, how are you?" I spoke to the clearly agitated airline ticket agent who stood in front of me with a disgruntled look on her face as she firmly grabbed my boarding ticket from my hand.

"Let's keep the line moving, you all will be debarking shortly. Ma'am, keep straight ahead, and your seat will be to the left, row C, thank you," she said, never making eye contact as she continued to rudely take tickets from passengers. I shook my head and exhaled as I found my seat. I placed my carry-on bag in the storage compartment over my head and took my seat next to the window.

I texted Khodi and reminded her of my arrival time before turning my phone on airplane mode. I connected to the complimentary Wi-Fi and browsed the web for restaurants near my landing spot.

"Ladies and gentlemen, my name is Suzanne, and I'm your chief flight attendant. On behalf of Captain Ronnie and the entire crew, welcome aboard South Delta Airlines flight 222, nonstop service from Atlanta, Georgia, to Newark, New Jersey.

"Our flight time will be two hours and fifteen minutes. We will be flying at an altitude of 16:30 meters at a ground speed of 550 miles per hour.

"At this time, make sure your seat backs and tray tables are in their full, upright position and that your seat belt is correctly fastened. Also, your portable electronic devices must be set to 'airplane' mode until an announcement is made upon arrival.

"We remind you that this is a non-smoking flight. Tampering with, disabling, or destroying the smoke detectors located in the lavatories is prohibited by law.

"You will find this and all other safety information in the card located in the seat pocket in front of you. We strongly suggest you read it before take-off. If you have any questions, please don't hesitate to ask one of our crew members. We wish you all an enjoyable flight."

I buckled my seatbelt across my lap as the flight attendant, Suzanne, continued. I placed my earphones in my ears and opened my Kindle app. I scrolled down to one of my favorite books by Ms. Grad Marie, Stealing the Heart of a Dirty South Hustla', and put it on read mode as I laid

my head back on my neck pillow and prepared for take-off.
I was finally ready to face the world on my own!

♥Chapter Two

GWOP

I sat at the table in the meeting room with a bottle of Hennessey in my hands and watched Bang as he spoke.

"OK, gang, this year, we have four major hits."

"Four major hits, gang," Sweetie repeated as she wrote our plan down on the dry erase board located behind my brother.

"Number one, we will be traveling to the great state of Texas. The massively populated city of Houston has a lot of goodies waiting for us." Sweetie grabbed the remote to the sixty-seven-inch smart TV that hung on the meeting room's wall and powered it on as he continued.

"As you all know, we will not be traveling together. Dr. Easy is already in route to assist anyone who may need medical attention. But you know what I always say, 'If there just happens to be any bloodshed, it better not be from any man—I'm sorry, Sweetie—or woman in our crew'." He laughed as Sweetie stood behind him and nodded.

I took the ice-cold bottle of Hennessey to my lips, sat back in my chair, and placed my eyes on the television screen as my brother spoke. I glanced around the table at the members of our crew. "Sweetie", a tall, blonde, Puerto Rican mami who was in her prime was from The Bronx, New York. She was our gofer and getaway driver. We also used her and her beauty to trap some of our potential targets to receive classified information from them. She was also my big brother Bang's cuddy buddy.

"Pilla the Hitta" was a twenty-one-year-old savage. He was fierce, violent, and uncontrolled. We recruited him one day about a year ago when Bang witnessed him stealing a pair of sneakers from a thug's feet who had just gotten shot down in cold blood by the owner of a bodega for trying to rob him. Mikey, better known as "Brains", was the Steven Q. Urkel of the clique. Even though he was only nineteen years old, he was a math magician. His brain was like an instant calculator. He could tell you the exact amount of a stack of money just by touching it. He accompanied me on most, but not all, my scopes of our planned heist, ten steps behind, of course. Mikey could be inside of a building for only seven minutes and tell you the dimensions of the spot and how many people were inside.

Dr. Easy was our own personal physician. He was a forty-year-old divorcee and a former neurologist surgeon who owned his own business. That was until he was found guilty of malpractice. He lost his wife and all his money, houses, and cars in a nasty divorce settlement. Since then, he'd been working under my brother and me. We needed him on our crew because if any of our soldiers suffered a wound, we couldn't just take them to an emergency room; we would have to reveal a truth about us that Bang had ordered we forever keep hidden.

My thirty-two-year-old brother, Aaron, better known as 'Bang', was four years older than me, and the boss of our clique. He set up all jobs, recruited members, and he decided what was to be distributed to each member. He got a kick out of taking from the government. The government of the United States of America was the largest gang, and they stole the most money through taxation, but the funny thing was, this country was founded to avoid taxation. Talk about an oxymoron.

Truthfully, we'd been taking back what had belonged to us all our lives. We were taught at a very early age how to rob people. Our parents, Christopher and Connie Thompson, were infamous bank robbers who were known as the modern-day Bonnie and Clyde. Sadly, nineteen years ago, they were murdered in cold blood during one of their many bank heists out in San Diego, California. My brother felt it was best to keep the family tradition alive, so we began our own squad to take back from the government what they had taken from us. Not just innocent and hardworking tax payer's money, but our dearly loved parents.

We never hit the same city or state, ever. That was the number one rule of being a successful thief: never leave a paper trail, and never get caught. And even though we'd made millions in our family business, we weren't flashy with our lifestyle or spending.

"Gwop!" Bang shouted, knocking me out of my thoughts. "Break the job down, brother." He leaned back in his chair and laughed as Sweetie took a seat in her usual spot during meetings: his lap. I cut my eyes at him, then scanned the table. The clicking noise Brain's nerdy ass was making against the table was starting to irk my nerves, so I jumped up, scaring the shit out of him and slammed my fist down on the table.

"Sorry, Gwop." He scarily smiled and slid the pen into his shirt pocket, then faced the TV so I could begin my presentation while the other members of our crew cracked up laughing at his geeky ass.

I walked around the table and stood next to the TV screen. I sipped from my bottle of Hennessey again, then passed it to my brother, who downed it quickly without stopping.

"OK, gang." I clapped my hands together and began to give them the details of our first job of the year. "We will be traveling to the great state of Texas. They say everything is bigger and better in Texas, and after my research, studies have shown that ding, ding, they are correct!

"We will be visiting Globe Finance, one of the largest loan companies in the world. I have received information from our inside man, Bradley Hartnabrig, the loan company's branch manager, that due to the holiday, there will be a large amount of untraceable Benjamins left behind in a vault. So, Mr. B. Hartnabrig and I have masterminded a daring plan to rob the vault—"

"So, Papi." Sweetie interrupted my presentation with her annoying, thick accent. She sounded just like Joseline from Love & Hip Hop: Atlanta. She had a bad-ass body and was a sweetheart, but I didn't see how Bang fucked her. I couldn't do it because, as soon as she opened that mouth of hers, a nigga's dick would go limp as fuck. I turned and gave her an agitated look. "When you chay a larsh amount? Ha much money we talking, baby?" she smiled.

"Brains break it down for her, bro," I ordered, then sat on the stool that was in front of the TV screen.

He let out an annoying, nerdy giggle, then pushed his glasses up the bridge of his nose and cleared his throat as he opened his laptop. "Well, after doing my calculations, the count that will be left in the vault before the after-holiday pick up will beeeeee… 300,000 big buckaroos!"

"Oh, hell yeah!" Pilla said as he pulled out his cell phone. "Shit, that's almost forty-two Gs a piece."

"Well, not actually, brother," Mikey began. "The total amount is 300,000 dollars, but after we take the thirty percent that our partner, B. Hartnabrig, is requesting, that will leave us with 210,000 dollars, and after splitting the remainder of that six ways, then the payout will be exactly 35,000 a piece. Oh yeah, minus the ten percent that Bang takes off top, so after that, we will make 31,500 dollars from this job." He ended and nodded to me so I could continue.

"Thirty-one thousand dollars? I can spend that down at the strip club," Pilla said and smacked his lips.

I stood up to continue and was interrupted again by Bang.

"Ay, homie, either you in or you in, because your dummy looking ass can get ghost right now. I'm helping you out. We have four jobs this year and believe me, they all gon' pay more than this one. I tried to negotiate with Hartnabrig and drop him down to twenty percent, but he refused, so whether you take this flight or not, we still going to get this money, with or without you." He looked at him and pointed his finger, then darted his eyes back at me.

"Damn, can I fucking continue without any more interruptions, please!" I gave him a sideways look as he held his hands up in surrender and nodded for me to continue.

"As I was fucking saying before being interrupted by you no-home-training-having idiots." I laughed as they snickered, knowing I meant no harm by my words.

"This three hunnit Gs will be locked away in the vault of Globe Finance. This money is prime for us to take because it is not going to or from a bank; it is simply recycled in the company and kept in the vault for their borrowers. I've received word from our Texas inside target connect, Hartnabrig, that the best day to do this heist would be the Saturday before Martin Luther King Day. The armored trucks are not scheduled to pick up the company's money until that Tuesday after the holiday. Limited employees are scheduled to work that day, and all other employees will be gone for the three-day weekend. The only catch is, we will only have twenty-six minutes to get into the office where the vault is, take what's ours, and get the fuck out of Texas."

"Twenty-six minutes? Papi, I drive with my stilettos, you know? I don't think I can—" Sweetie started, but Bang kissed her lips to make her hush her annoying-ass mouth and motioned with his hand for me to continue.

"Gon' 'head and break it down to us, Brains," Pilla said as he looked at Mikey.

Mikey snickered and pulled at his shirt collar before he stood up to take the floor.

Steven Q. Urkel looking ass nigga. I laughed to myself.

****

Two hours later, our meeting was adjourned, and we split, going our separate ways to embark on our greed journey in the great state of Texas. Even though Brains was an annoying nerd, most of the time, whenever we traveled, he was always close to me, following a few steps behind to be unnoticeable, of course. We arrived at the New Jersey transit station to head to the airport. Bang texted everyone to remind us of the game plan and our meeting spot when we got to our destination. As I hopped on the train, a thick-ass shorty who was pulling two big suitcases bumped into me on her way out. I stopped and mugged her ass up and down. I could tell by the look on her face she was scared by my reaction.

"Oh, excuse me. I am so sorry." She smiled, squinting her beautiful light-brown eyes and showing her pretty-ass pearly white teeth. I could tell by her thick country accent that she had to be from the south. I looked her up and down again and nodded, getting a perfect view of that fat ass booty she had when she walked off. She had cream-colored skin and long, sandy brown hair that was tucked underneath a fitted cap into a ponytail. I couldn't stand when people from different parts of the world visited our area. They were all clueless fools who were in the way. Fucking tourists! I thought and shook my head. I took my seat on the train and went over the plan in my head again. Truth is, I was secretly getting tired of doing these jobs. I loved the huge payouts, but I was knocking on thirty years old, and I wanted to be a successful business owner one day. But I wouldn't dare speak on this to my stubborn-ass brother. I knew he wasn't going for me trying to go legit. He loved taking from the government. He said if he had to rob motherfuckers blind for every year we'd been without our parents, he would.

I remember growing up in the busy streets of Elizabeth, New Jersey, as a child. We grew up poor and lived in a small two-bedroom apartment. My father worked down at the local post office, and my mother was a stay-at-home mother and wife who spent most of her mornings sitting on the stoop, sipping coffee and gossiping with Mrs. Williams, another young housewife who lived in our building. We didn't have everything as kids growing up, but our parents made sure we had all the essentials, and we never went hungry.

Our father, Christopher, worked at the local post office in Linden, New Jersey, for almost twelve years before he was let go. After many years of early mornings and late nights, being overworked and underpaid, they let my father go. He explained to my mother that he was informed that several employees would lose their jobs due to the government making cuts. This news destroyed my father. He went through a deep depression for almost three weeks. He didn't eat, bathe or sleep.

Usually, after a successful day down at the office, he and Mr. Williams, who we called "Uncle Rob", would sit in our family room and knock back a couple of cold brews while watching sports, or the nightly news on television, but since the job separation, both men were distant from each other. I remember one night when I couldn't sleep, I went downstairs to get a cold drink and I overheard my father and Uncle Rob talking. I tip-toed down the cold wooden steps that led from my and my brother's room. Both men were standing over our kitchen table, looking at a map of New Jersey.

I stood in the corner of the hallway and listened to their conversation.

"I'm telling you, we can do this, man!" I looked over at Uncle Rob, who stood there shaking his head while he gave my father a confused look.

"We busted our fucking asses down at that job for years, and now they want to let us go? Think about it! It's time for us to take back what the government took from us. Our income, our respect as men. Our fucking dignity!" my father's deep voice boomed through the house.

"Just let me get some time to sleep on it, OK?" Uncle told my father.

"All right, two days!" he shouted as he held up two fingers in front of his friend's face. "Two days. After that, I'm pulling the heist with or without cha!"

"All right, Chrissy, I'll get back at cha," Uncle Rob said before making his way to the hallway to exit. He stopped in his tracks and turned my way when he caught me in the hallway, eavesdropping.

"Aye, D, what are you doing up, little man?" he asked, walking my way and squatting his large frame down to my height.

"I—I couldn't sleep, so I was coming to get a drink," I admitted in a shaky voice. I was almost eight years old at the time, and I knew that my best bet was to get back upstairs to bed before I upset my strict father. Our parents were always kind to us, but since my father's job separation, he had a very unpleasant mood around us, so our mother told us to stay clear when possible. My father's colleague left our home and made the short distance across the hall to his residence as I turned to make my way back up the creaky wooden stairs that led to me and my older brother's bedroom.

"D, come here, son." My father's deep baritone voice stopped me in my tracks. I wiped my sweaty palms on my Superman pajama bottoms before I made my way to the small kitchen table where he sat with both elbows on the table, and his right hand rested on his forehead.

"Yea, Pop?" I called to him while standing opposite of where he sat. He extended his arm to me, motioning me to take a seat, and I did as prompted. He passed me a small yellow cup that was filled with water. I licked my lips before exhaling. I quenched my thirst with the quickness, swallowing the cool liquid that was cupped in my hands.

I thanked my father, then stood and placed the cup in the kitchen sink before turning to exit. He grabbed me by the back of my thick pajama shirt and swallowed me in his swollen arms, holding me tightly. "You know I love you, son," he sniffled, tightening his already firm grip around my small frame. We were always taught men weren't supposed to cry, but from the crack in my father's voice at this moment, I didn't know how I felt about that.

"I love you, too, Pop," I responded and wrapped my petite hands around his muscular frame. The short years I had been on this earth, not one time had I ever seen my father this emotional. His face was red, his eyes were weary. Our father was a large man, standing almost six feet four, and he had a muscular build. My older brother Aaron got his fair skin complexion from our father, and I was dark like our mother.

"I'm going to fix this. I promise. I'm going to always support my family, even if I have to die trying." He stared into my eyes. I nodded and hugged him again with my right arm while I brushed away the light tears that began to fall from my eyes with my left.

♥

I snapped out of my thoughts and focused on my brother as he tapped the watch on his wrist. "All right, crew, are y'all ready?" he shouted and looked over his shoulder at me and Pilla, who were squatted in the back of our gofers getaway van, ready to jump out and handle business.

"Twenty-six minutos, Papi!" Sweetie exclaimed as she pulled to the back door of Globe Finance.

"Aye, boss," Mikey's squeaky voice blasted through our radio. "It's time… Go!" he screamed through our speaker, and like clockwork, we pulled our black ski masks over our faces and jumped out of the van as Sweetie slowly drove through the alley. Bang snatched the back door open, and we followed him down the hallway in search of our inside men and women who posed as hostages. I watched Pilla as he shoved his flare rifle in an elderly woman's face, which made her old ass instantly piss on herself. I tried to hold in my laughter and continued to walk down the hallway until I reached our inside target, Mr. Hartnabrig's, office. I shoved my pistol in his face and demanded he lead me to the company's vault.

"Come on, you don't have to be so rough, Mr. Robber Man." Hartnabrig snickered as he looked over his shoulder. He squatted down and entered the six-digit code on the keypad and slowly opened the door. My mouth watered on a dime as I stared at the bundle of dead presidents. I threw the large, black duffle bag at his feet and he began to fill it up. I looked at my watch and saw that we had less than fifteen minutes to leave Globe Finance and make it back to the airport for a successful getaway.

"Hurry up, Hartnabrig," I whispered to him as I heard a siren ringing above my head. Soon, two gunshots were fired. My brother Bang ran up behind me, snatched the duffle bag, and made his way out the door we had come in. We skidded down the alley in search of our getaway driver. When she pulled up, we hopped in the van as she weaved in and out of the busy downtown traffic. Bang switched the radio from Sweetie's usual hip-hop and tuned in to the local news station.

"Just a few minutes ago, in Downtown Houston, the lending company Globe Finance's vault was robbed. The amount that was taken has not been identified as of yet, and police are arriving now to the scene as this will be a continued investigation." The news anchor continued.

I sat with my back against the inside of the van and looked over at my brother, who was across from me smiling as he switched the Benjamins from the black duffle bag into a small suitcase. I helped him cover the money with clothes, changed my outfit, and zipped the suitcase up. Sweetie pulled into the airport's parking garage, and I hopped out with the loaded suitcase and made my way to check in. Sally, the check-in attendant, smiled at me as soon as she saw me heading her way.

"Hello, sir, you made it just in time. Take off is in twenty minutes." She smiled at me as we swapped suitcases. Sally was another one of our inside workers. The percentage Bang took off of everyone's pay paid the team who helped us with our successful getaway. I nodded to her and smiled as she ripped the stub from my ticket, and I walked down the long corridor to take my seat on the plane. I placed the small suitcase above my head in the carry-on storage bin and took my seat. I nodded to Pilla as he walked onto the plane and took a seat on the row to the right of me. I sat back and exhaled, preparing myself for the three-hour nap I would enjoy on the way home.

♥Chapter Three

BANG

"Aaayyyeee, Papi!" Sweetie moaned as she sat in between my legs with her neon pink, blinged-out, hump nails wrapped firmly around my hard dick. She pulled out a pack of our magic dust and sprinkled some on her tongue, then wrapped her pretty, pink lips around my mushroom tip. I rolled my eyes to the back of my head as she swallowed every inch of me down her moist throat. My manhood dug deeper into her pleasurable tunnel with each graze of her tongue as it massaged my flesh. Sweetie was a fine mami from the city, and not only was she my crew's getaway driver, but she was also my li'l honey dip on the side. I wasn't in love with Sweetie, but I had mad love for her because I knew she had my back with no questions asked.

I first met her about three years ago, right after a small job I hit in Kentucky. I had just robbed an ACE check cashing office, moments after the money truck left the parking lot from filling up their safe with crispy dead presidents. I didn't notice that when I pulled up to hit the spot, my dumb ass had parked in a tow-away zone. So, after the assistant manager, with my gun to her head, filled my duffle bag with the fresh deposit from their safe, I hauled ass out the back door. When I ran down the small alley located in the back of the office buildings, I noticed when I peeked around the corner of the building, my damn hoopty was being hooked up to the tow truck.

My adrenaline rushed to my head as I searched the nearby parking lots for a way to get out. I ran down the feeder road of the busy freeway until I reached the parking lot of a fast food place. I ran around the lot, peeking in windows of parked cars to see if some dumb ass had left their shit unlocked or running so I could make my escape, but I had no luck. I panicked and ran to the back of the parking lot as a small Jeep sped through and drove to the speaker box to place their food order. I reached my arm through the passenger window that was cracked and popped the lock, then slid in and put the barrel of my pistol to the fine bitch's forehead. " Drive, bitch, and don't say shit!" I barked at her.

She pulled a gun out of thin air and pointed it at me. "Now, you're going to wait until I order my fucking meal first, Papi!" she snapped back at me. I must admit, she had a nigga's dick tingling hard in my sweats. I nodded and let her place her order while shaking my head. I held my hands up in surrender and nodded for her to continue. "Can I get a larsh strawberry and banana milkshake with extra whip cream, because I like it creamy!" She laughed and looked my way. "You want something, Papi?" she asked with raised eyebrows. I laughed to myself while shaking my head.

"Nah, shorty. I'm good, yo."

"Suit yourself." She shrugged. "That will be all, love." She whipped her Jeep around to the pick-up window. Sirens sounded loudly behind us from a line of police cars who were speeding down the highway towards the spot I'd just hit.

"Fuck, fuck, fuck!" I shouted.

"Mami, I really need you to put your foot to that pedal and—" I stopped my words when I saw that shorty was already steps ahead of me. She snatched her shake from the cashier, leaving her change, and hauled ass out of the restaurant's parking lot.

"Shit!" she cursed as she jumped from lane to lane on US 119, swerving her Jeep to avoid hitting innocent drivers. "I knew I shouldn't have stopped for this fucking shake. Damn it!" she yelled to herself as she continued driving like a maniac. I looked over my shoulder and noticed that besides the many cars on the slightly busy highway, it was clear of police. My eyes scanned the backseat that was full of bags of clothes and shoes.

"Mami, you a booster or something? You driving like crazy and ain't no pigs behind us, shorty." I laughed at her.

She glanced in the rearview mirror and exhaled, then pulled into an abandoned parking lot at the next exit on the feeder road. She pulled up to a small black car and hopped out. I sat in awe as I witnessed her slid a jimmy in the car's window and pop the lock before hopping in the driver's seat to hotwire it. She ran back to the Jeep and began to grab the stolen merchandise from the back seat. "I don't know what to tell you, Papi, but you're on your own now. I gotta get back to the city."

"Wait, ma. I-I lost my car during my job. Which way you headed? I'll see if my brother can meet up with us." I begged her because I really didn't know what to do at the time. I didn't want to be stuck in fucking Kentucky, especially with all this money on me. "Look, I'll even pay you." I persuaded her by pulling out a crispy stack of greenbacks. She looked me up and down again while standing with folded arms before nodding in agreeance. We slid into the car and headed back to our city.

On the eleven-hour drive back home, we had more than enough time to properly introduce ourselves, and I let her in on what I did for a living and how I could definitely use her services for each job after witnessing the way she had handled the freeway earlier. She was fine, sassy, and real as fuck. She had a strong attitude and didn't take any shit, and that's the reason she was my Sweetie.

The way she slurped spit off my hard shaft made my eyes roll into the back of my head. I was almost at my climax until it was quickly interrupted by my incoming text message tone. I was mad as fuck. I hoped it wasn't any of my workers from the heist we'd pulled today. My crew knew after every payout, I was unavailable until the next meeting. I opened the text message and exhaled while shaking my head.

Bitter Bitch: I see your job was successful. So, when can I be expecting you to come by?

I blew air out of my nose, which instantly made my blonde beauty stand to her feet as she wiped her mouth. She could tell by my facial expression and my dick that was growing soft that I was frustrated.

"Es OK, Papi. Just call me later." Sweetie chunked me the deuce as she made her exit.

Me: Man, I'm on my way.

I was tired of giving my money to this bitch to hush her fucking mouth.

♥

When I pulled up to the meeting spot and saw the evil smirk plastered on this greedy bitch's face, my stomach twisted in knots. She opened my passenger door and slid into the seat, trying to rub her hands up my leg to my dick, but I gently brushed it away.

"So, that's how you acting today? What you wildin' and shit for? Yo' light skin ass wasn't acting like that the other day when a bitch was swallowing yo' motherfucking dick!" She laughed while crossing her arms over her chest and giving me a sideways look.

"Look, shorty, it's just been a long day, that's all. A nigga is fuckin' tied. I'm ready to go home and rest, shit." I softly brushed my hand down the side of her face to ease her agitation. I couldn't stand this bitch, but she looked out for my crew and me on every heist we took on, so, that was the only reason I dealt with her. I was already giving this dictmatized hoe a percentage of my cut, but this freaky bitch wanted dick every time I saw her. I just wasn't in the mood. I looked down at my cell phone screen at an incoming call from my brother, Gwop.

"Look, this my girl. I gotta get to the crib, ma." I lied to her as I passed her a small, brown paper bag with her portion from the job inside it.

She snatched the bag and hopped out of my car with an attitude, not closing the door. I shook my head and leaned over to close the passenger door. I silently thanked GOD above for saving me from this horny hoe; I wasn't with her shit today.

♥Chapter Four

SHIRI

When I stepped off the train, my stomach immediately twisted up in knots. I wasn't sure if my queasiness was from the fast speed the train traveled or the horrid smell of death at the train station.

When I saw Khodi, I had a few choice words for her. I told her days in advance what time my plane would be arriving, and she tells me at the last minute she can't pick me up from the airport because she was working late. I was frightened the whole time during my train ride. This was my first time on the east coast alone since a few months back when I traveled up with my parents to check out the condo complex, I would be living in. Being from the South, I was used to kind people with Southern hospitality, but I could see all the home training my parents had taught me was out the window now. I feared for my life when I accidentally bumped into a man earlier when exiting the train. If looks could kill, I would've been dead on arrival.

I looked at my phone and followed the path my GPS gave me to wait for Khodi. When my phone lit up from her incoming call, I felt a huge sigh of relief. "Please tell me you're close?" I begged her while examining my surroundings of the busy people who sped walked all around me, heading to their known destinations while I stood, lost and confused, at the train station. I exhaled deeply while I waited for my best friend's reply. Maybe I should've thought about this before trying to be grown and jumping off the porch already, I thought. I really wanted my mommy.

"Relax, bestie, I'm pulling up behind you now." She soothed my anxiousness as I turned around and saw her small Benz SUV pull up.

A wide smile spread across my face, and I excitedly pulled my rolling suitcase down the ramp and ran to my best friend, who stood with opened arms. When I approached her car, I let go of my suitcases that trailed behind me and pulled her tightly into my arms. I missed my best friend dearly, and this was my first time seeing her in almost six months since the last time she'd visited home in Atlanta.

"I'm so excited you're here, bestie!" she exclaimed while helping me load my belongings into the back of her truck. "So, how was your flight?" She looked at me with a sly grin as she threw her car in drive and drove down the street to enter the busy freeway. I turned my nose up at her and shook my head.

"The flight was cool, but that train station was horrible!" I cut my eyes at her. "That's why I told you weeks in advance when I would be landing so you could pick me up from the airport on time, Khodisha She'nae Roberts!" I playfully shouted at her while pulling out my cell to check for nearby restaurants to ease my growling tummy.

"Aw, I'm really sorry, friend. I got caught up down at the office. Last minute paperwork I had to get together before the holiday." She tapped my shoulder and gave me a sad puppy-dog face as she merged onto the busy freeway.

"I guess I can forgive you, if and only if you take me to get something to eat. I'm starving!"

"Yes! I know the perfect place with gourmet Asian cuisine. Dragonfly!"

"Dragonfly, what the hell is that?" I asked Khodi with a confused look.

"Don't worry. You'll love it." She smiled and took the next exit off the freeway. "Then it's Thursday, so it's gonna be jumping tonight."

I crossed my arms and gave her the side-eye. She knew I didn't step on the club scene like that. And after my bump-in with Mr. Sexual Chocolate earlier, I wasn't so sure I wanted to party east coast style because these motherfuckers were rude as hell. This was definitely not what I was used to.

"Girl, I've been on a plane all day. I'm not dressed to go to a damn club. And I'm hungry. Can I get a raincheck? I just want to eat and get settled in. Maybe we can go out tomorrow." She nodded and agreed as we pulled up to the restaurant she'd mentioned earlier. I hesitated before getting out the car. I pulled down the visor mirror to refresh my lip gloss and brushed back the loose hairs on my forehead underneath my cap.

"Come on, Ri, you look fine, mama. It's still early, and people are still having dinner. It doesn't start getting packed until later. Let's go eat, you'll love the food," she promised.

I trusted my dear friend and followed her into the restaurant. She was my best friend, so she knew what I liked and disliked. We were thick as thieves growing up. Our fathers would call us Milli Vanilli because I had fair skin and green eyes like my mother, and Khodi had the most beautiful dark chocolate skin. My friend stood just a few inches shorter than me at five feet four inches, and she had the thickest, waviest, jet-black hair that she preferred to wear straight. Like myself, she was the apple of her father's eye, and she was the middle child of three girls. Khodi grew up in the same top of the line schools I did, and she also had strict parents. But one thing I loved about her is, she is very rebellious. She did things with no hesitation and lived her life on the edge. She wasn't scared to try new things in life, and that was what made her make this major move to the tri-state area.

We walked inside, and I was surprised by how nice the restaurant looked. The hostess greeted Khodi by name and followed us to the large rectangular bar that sat in the middle of the restaurant. The hostess pulled out the dark-brown leather high chairs for each of us to sit and handed us a menu. My eyes widened as I scanned the wonderful descriptions and pictures that were listed of the restaurant's dishes. Asian cuisine was my absolute favorite kind of food; my bestie knew what she was doing. I was glad she was making me feel comfortable after such an uncomfortable arrival.

"Friennndd, the Thai chili wings are so delish! Let's get those for an appetizer, and they have some good-ass sesame chicken lettuce wraps you will love."

When our perfectly garnished entrees arrived at the table, my mouth instantly watered. Everything looked just as good as it tasted, and the Asian pear martinis we had tasted like they were made from heaven. I still couldn't believe I was finally starting my adult life.

"Ahhhhhh!" he moaned.

"Uh-uh, nigga. Take this shit. Mmmnn. Yes, daddy!" Khodi screamed from inside her bedroom. I grabbed the pillow I was lying on from the couch and covered my ears to drown out her screams. She and her "company" had been going all night and were currently on round three. She explained to me earlier while we were having dinner at the restaurant that, unfortunately, my condo wouldn't be ready until Monday. At first, I didn't mind because it would be my first night sleeping alone in my life, and I wasn't sure I was ready to do that just yet. But if I had known my best friend had a scheduled fuck session tonight, I would've told her to drop me off at the nearest hotel. I admit I was a tad bit jealous because it was going on nine months since me and my on-again-off-again boyfriend Byron had been intimate.

I was more turned on by the noises from the porn scene I was sure was going down in my best friend's bedroom. When her mate slapped her ass, I couldn't take it anymore. I jumped up from the couch and tiptoed to the bedroom door, softly placing my ear on it. I closed my eyes and imagined I was Khodi, currently getting my back beat in. I went to my suitcase and pulled out my small satin bag that I usually kept my pocket-sized lipstick vibrator in. I was glad TSA hadn't confiscated it earlier at the airport because I needed to get this pent-up frustration out of my system.

I jumped back on the couch and covered my body with my favorite hot pink blanket. I lifted my night shirt up above my breasts, showing off my erect nipples which instantly turned me on even more. I slid my satin panties down to my ankles and spread my legs, pulling my thick lower lips open, and sliding in the vibrating satisfaction fulfilling my craving. The more my friend and her freaky partner moaned, the deeper I dug into my creamy center to please myself.

My mind traveled back to the last time I was intimate with a man. I was a virgin when Byron and I got together, as was he, so the three times we made love was simple and boring. Basically, in missionary position. Having Khodisha as my best friend, she always let me in on her many sexcapades with her multiple partners. Unlike myself, she wasn't shy. She had always been the outgoing and outspoken one between the two of us. She did who she wanted and what she wanted, despite what anyone had to say about it, her parents included.

After I erupted like a Hawaiian volcano, I went into the guest bathroom to freshen up and hide my self-pleasuring evidence down in the bottom of my suitcase. On the way out of the bathroom, Khodi's bedroom door swung open and out walked a muscular, statuesque man with deep, wavy hair that connected to a perfectly tapered beard that complemented his medium dark skin. He looked me up and down as he glided across the cool marble floors and made his way to the refrigerator. I tried to stop my eyes from staring at his nicely chiseled body. The way his checkered pajamas drooped from his body, showcasing his V underneath his abs that led to his manhood made me cream on myself. I walked back to the couch and buried myself under the covers, hoping my friend and Mr. Sexual Chocolate would be going for another round soon because I would be ready again with my lipstick vibrator. Especially now, since I had a perfect visual of Mr. Loud and Freaky. I couldn't wait until I met one of these east coast niggas who could knock the dust off this pussy. I needed it bad.

Chapter Five

SHIRI

Like the spoiled brat I was, I called my father so he could use his status to expedite the process of getting my condo together. I loved my best friend Khodi with all my heart, but low-key, I was jealous of her getting dick every night when I had no one to beat my back in. It felt great to finally be on my own. I could do as I pleased, with who I pleased, without my parents' say so.

It was now Monday morning, and my first day of work at my new job, so after moonwalking to "Dirty Diana" by Michael Jackson across my custom-made marble floors, it was time to get dressed. I skimmed through the clothes that hung in my large walk-in closet. I decided on an ivory-colored, ruffled satin blouse and matched it with a knee-length, vintage Burberry skirt. I draped a black, sheer mini shawl across my shoulders, and threw on my camel-colored ankle booties before refreshing my lip gloss and meeting Khodi downstairs in the foyer to ride with her to the office.

"Look at you. Ms. 'Southern Bell' slaying and shit!" My best friend joked with me, and I playfully turned around, showing off my outfit for the day.

♥

Almost thirty minutes later, we pulled up to the employee parking garage at Tri-State Financial. I stepped out the truck and slid the strap of my Louis Vuitton business bag on my shoulder and followed my friend onto the elevator. I was nervously excited about my new job. I'd heard nothing but good things about this branch, and I was more than ready to join the company. We reached the third floor, and I quickly finished the rest of the strawberry-banana smoothie I had made for breakfast to settle the jumping butterflies that filled my stomach. I looked over at my bestie, who smiled and nodded while motioning for me to join her in the conference room that was down the hall.

"Have a seat right here. I'll be right back after I drop some things off at my desk and check my morning messages. Mr. Jenkins should be coming in shortly to go over the safety and security procedures with you and to have you fill out all the new hire paperwork." She tapped me on the shoulder again before making her exit. I looked behind me and gave a faint smile to the busy employees who passed the glass windows of the room I sat in.

When our head supervisor, Mr. Ronald Jenkins, came in to greet me, I immediately felt uncomfortable as he undressed me with his eyes. Mr. Jenkins was an older Puerto Rican gentleman who was surprisingly attractive for his age. His salt and pepper, tightly coiled hair was cut into a nice taper fade, and his deep-caved dimples added to his handsomeness. He gave me a quick tour of the branch, then showed me to my office. I was glad when he did so I could hide from his googly eyes for the next couple of hours.

♥

♥Two Weeks Later…

I exhaled and began to empty the items from my work bag and load up my new desk. I was very proud of myself for becoming a woman and adult by venturing off to start a new life without my parents controlling every minute of it. I looked up and saw Khodi speaking with a customer who had just walked in our branch. This brother was fine as fuck. I couldn't see the front of his face, but from the side, he had smooth, dark chocolate skin, his shoulder-length dreadlocks were braided back in two big plaits, and his tailored suit hugged his chiseled body perfectly. Even though he was dressed exquisitely, I could tell by his swag he had probably graduated from some block in the hood. This was the East Coast, though, so pretty much everyone had swag.

After filling up my desk, I stood and straightened out my skirt before walking towards where my best friend and Mr. Fine were standing, when I was interrupted by our supervisor, who called me to his office. Damn it, Ri! I said to myself as my pussy purred in between my thick thighs. I needed to get a new boo soon so I could have consistent dick because my vibrator had given out on me the other night. May she rest in pieces.

"Coming, Mr. Jenkins!" I said over my shoulder with a sarcastic smile plastered on my face. Since I had been working here, this nigga had been annoying the fuck out of me.

♥Chapter Six

GWOP

"I'm telling you, baby. Just one more, one more job and we can be done with this," my father persuaded my mother, Connie.

"You said that last time, Chrissy. Now, I understand why you wanted to pull off the first job, but I really didn't think you would make a career out of robbing people, Hun. I want no more parts of it, I'm out."

"Well, I'll be in Cali in the morning, with or without ya, babe. They owe us! Everything they took from us—"

"You know I love you dearly, but the truth is, it doesn't matter how many heists we pull, the government will ALWAYS win!"

My father stormed out of the family room and brushed past me on the staircase to pack for his job in the morning, not noticing me. I tip-toed down the stairs and slowly walked into the room where my mother sat in my father's recliner, weeping.

"Mommy, what's wrong?" I asked in my sweet, innocent voice, then climbed into her lap and tightly wrapped my small arms around her neck. She began to rub small circles on my back and attempted to dry her tears.

"I just want you to know, D, that if anything ever happens to me, always remember that Mommy loves you. I love you both!" she exclaimed. Her eyes welled up with tears as she pulled my brother Aaron, who had crept up behind where we were sitting, into our embrace.

"I know, Mommy. I know," my brother said and squeezed our mother tightly.

Little did we know, that would be our last time seeing our mother alive. Every time our parents went to do a job out of state, we stayed at home with our mother's father who we called Pop-Pop.

See, we were street niggas, but we had plenty of book sense. We had gained that from our mother's father. Pop-Pop was a genius when it came to business and economics. Shit, I wouldn't have been able to pass my high school government class without him. He taught us everything we needed to know about this crooked-ass system we had to deal with on a daily, and that was why it was so easy for us to beat it.

The next morning, our grandfather called us downstairs to have our routine morning breakfast. I washed up and scurried downstairs. My job was to turn on the morning news while Pop-Pop loaded our plates with food, and my big brother set the table. I made my way to the kitchen table to take a seat while our grandfather walked my way with our plates in his hands, but he halted and stared at the television. Aaron looked him up and down, then did an about-face towards the Tv. His eyes grew wide, and he stood like a deer caught in headlights. I was only eight years old at the time and didn't understand much about what was going on in the world, but I knew something wasn't right by the shocked expression on Pop-Pop's face.

Our grandfather had fair skin, as did our mother and my older brother, and at this time, his face was fluorescent, as if he had seen a ghost. He set our breakfast down on the corner of the table which caused the plates to fall and shatter and rushed to the living room. I walked up behind him and saw my father, Christopher Thompson, standing in the middle of the street with a pistol to his right temple, and fear in his eyes, shaking his head. The SWAT team surrounded him with their rifles drawn. There were loose Benjamin Franklins scattered all over the street and the trunk of my parents' 1970 white-and-black-striped El Camino.

The news anchor began to speak…

"Hello, I am Susan Mc Daniel, reporting live from Capital Financial here in San Diego, California, where a robbery has just taken place. Police have identified the suspects as Christopher and Connie Thompson, all the way from Linden, New Jersey. At this time, police have the last living suspect, Mr. Thompson, surrounded, and are asking him to surrender so no additional bloodshed takes place. This heist took a turn for the worse when Mrs. Thompson attempted to flee from the police. Shots were fired, unfortunately, causing her to be fatally injured."

I swallowed the lump in my throat and kneeled in front of the television, unmoving. Pop-Pop sat in my father's recliner and shook his head, and my brother ran to the large couch and pulled out my father's gun and pointed it at the TV. "I'm gonna kill them! I'm going to kill them all for killing Mommy!" he cried. Our grandfather grabbed the pistol from my eleven-year-old brother's hands and disarmed it. He scooped him into his arms, and we all continued to watch the demise of our parents as our eyes welled up with tears.

The negotiator asked for my father to surrender his weapon, but he refused. He turned and walked to the car, which my mother's deceased body sat in, and opened the driver's door. He lifted her slumped body from the seat and placed one last kiss on her lips before closing the door and opening fire into the crowd of policemen and women who surrounded him. They fired back multiple shots, causing my father's defeated body to slowly hit the cold, hard concrete as his soul departed it.

Seeing some shit like that at such an early age fucked a nigga up for life. I never wanted to have kids because God forbid, we ever got caught up out here in these streets, I would never want my seeds to witness that bullshit. These white folks didn't give a hot damn about ending black lives; to them, only blue lives mattered.

I exhaled and pulled down Main Street in Berkeley Heights, New Jersey. At our last meeting, Bang let the crew know that our upcoming heist would be the best and biggest one we'd ever had. At first, I was against it because it was too close to home. The only reason I agreed to go through with this job was because I planned on calling it quits afterward. I wanted to pack up and leave the east coast and start a new life somewhere else in this crazy world. Who knows. I could probably meet a fly shorty who was worthy of loving a hood nigga like me. This robbing shit was becoming ill to a nigga. I wanted revenge for my parents just as my brother and grandfather did, but I felt like we had stolen enough, and now it was time to enjoy our life instead of living in secret and looking over our shoulders every single day.

I pulled up to the curb around the corner from the bank, parked the rental I used when I wanted to be incognegro during my case-outs and hopped out. I was dressed down in a custom-tailored, dark-grey, Gucci slim fitted suit, with sky blue Giuseppe loafers that matched my undershirt to a T. I had my stylist braid my long dreads that hung to the middle of my back into two braids.

"Aye, Gwop!" Mikey screeched into my earpiece, which made me rip it out instantly. I could hear him rambling continually when I replaced the earpiece in my right ear.

"Brains, I'm not deaf, you know?" I chastised him with a slight smirk as I heard him let out his signature annoying, nerdy giggle.

"Sorry, boss man," he snickered and turned down his mic's volume. "Your lapel camera isn't coming in clear. All we can see are your size twelve Gucci loafers." His laughter was joined by my brother's. I shook my head as I walked around the corner and up the steep steps of the large bank. I tugged at my collar to fix the camera's view and waited for an all-clear from my crew who was parked across the street in one of our getaway vans before I pulled the door open and strutted in.

Almost immediately, I was greeted by a short, bad-built honey who had long Peruvian bundles that hung to her flat ass. She smiled in my face, showing off her green contacts that, paired with her dark skin, made her look like a damn X-Box system. Shorty wasn't ugly, but she wasn't my type, either. I liked all-natural females, the ones with their own hair, nails, and eyes. A lot of these chicks out here couldn't score a good man because they tried so hard to keep up with the in-crowd, but a real nigga liked his woman au naturale.

"Hello, I am the acting branch manager for today, assistant supervisor Khodisha Roberts. How may I help you today, sir?" Li'l long weave, flat booty asked me again. I heard her speaking, but I was distracted by another employee. The way her wide hips swayed from side to side as she glided in her dark-grey Kate Spade pencil skirt that matched my suit. Her Red Bottoms lightly clicked on the mosaic tile floors as she strutted across them on her way back to her office. I was glad she had her hair pinned up in a tight bun because it gave me a wonderful view of her fat ass. When she reached her desk and took a seat behind it, raising her bedazzled mug of caffeine crack to her perfectly, pink-painted lips, my soldier instantly saluted. I might forget a name, but never a fat ass booty.

"Earth to Darren Thompson!" Bang shouted in my earpiece, snapping me back to reality.

"Oh, yes, ma'am. I'm so sorry. Yes, I'm here to see about opening up a business account." I smiled at her, making her blush.

"I'll be more than happy to help you out with that today, sir. If you could follow me down this hallway to my office." I followed nappy, long back down the long hallway, trying hard not to look at Ms. Southern Booty as we walked past her office. Good thing she had her head down because I didn't want her to see this monster that was waving at her through my pants. I didn't want my brother in my business. Every time we cased out a bank, his ass was parked outside somewhere, waiting for a nigga to fuck up. She was thick, so she probably couldn't take dick anyway, I thought.

♥

"OK, crew, for our next job, we will be traveling to Cali baby!" Bang exclaimed as he stood in front of the dry erase board in the meeting room. I had a slight hangover from the night before, so I didn't understand why this light skinned ass nigga was so got damn loud at nine in the damn morning. "Our next job, our next job will be the local post office in Acampo, California—" Bang continued before he was interrupted by Pilla.

"Yo, a post office?" he questioned with a confused look, then burst out laughing, making my brother dart his eyes at him.

I smirked and kept my eyes on my brother while he finished his presentation. "Yea, nigga, a fucking post office!" his voice boomed towards Pilla's li'l ignorant ass. I was growing tired of the tension between the two of them, and I was sure the rest of the crew was as well.

"Our inside target is the general manager of all branches of the small populated town—"

"I'm just saying, what the fuck we jackin' from a post office, nigga, the stamps?" Pilla joked, interrupting him again, which brought the whole meeting room to laughter, including me. Truthfully, I agreed with him because I didn't understand exactly what we could gain from a damn post office, but I knew my big brother was about his cheddar, so I knew it would benefit us all.

"Brains! Break it down, homie," Bang shouted.

The freaky geek stood up, straightened out the collar on his Ralph Lauren tee, and took the floor.

"OK, ladies," he said while looking at Sweetie and Pilla. "And gentlemen," he said, looking me and Bang's way.

"No, we won't be jackin' stamps," Brains mimicked Pilla, agitating him even more as he rocked side to side in his chair and exhaled deeply.

"Even though this small city has a population of only 341 people. We got word from a friend of mine that someone accidentally on purpose ordered too many cases of money orders. Ten, to be exact." He snickered in his nerdy voice.

"Now, I happen to know a guy who has a machine that specializes in making blank one's worth so much more with a touch of a few buttons. Each case of money orders has a total of 250 blank copies inside worth up to 1,000 dollars each. Since there are a total of ten extra cases… this woo—" He clutched his chest, mimicking the late Fred Sanford. "This job will pay two point five… million big buckaroos!!"

When Brains dropped that dollar amount, my dick tingled. I looked over at Sweetie, who, for the first time in her life, didn't have anything to say as she sat on my brother's lap in shock, playing with the calculator in her phone. "Wait, th-that's 416,000?" she turned to ask Bang with wide eyes.

"Well, 350,000 after taxes, fees and interest." He nodded and laughed. She wrapped her hands tightly around his neck and shoved her tongue down his throat.

"I'll be glad when we no longer have to pay the taxes, fees and interest," Pilla mumbled before placing a bottle of water to his lips. Like the speed of light, Bang hopped up from his seat, knocking Sweetie to the floor, and slapped the bottle right from Pilla's lips, then snatched him up by his collar.

"You got something you want to say to me, nigga? Don't mumble, say that shit loud and clear where I can hear you, homie." My brother threatened him as he laughed in his face. Mikey jumped in between the two angry men, attempting to calm them down.

I stepped up from my seat at the table to break them up. "Come on now, we been doing this together too long to be fighting over some fucking money. We better than that. Calm down, brother. Everybody be cool, OK?" I stared at my brother, who was the spitting image of my mother, who I missed so much. His fair skin turned bright red when he was angry, just as hers had every time she and my father got into an argument.

Finally, I was able to calm them down, and we continued our meeting before heading off to Cali the next day to cop that 2.5 mil.

♥

I took in my surroundings as Sweetie drove down the long dirt roads of Acampo. This town was small and resembled a little Mexico. When we first started our family business years ago, we would only hit small, country towns like this one. In a small town, everybody knew each other, most were family members or close friends, and many people kept their homes unlocked because it was safe. In small cities, the residents never expected anything bad to happen, and that was what made them an easier target. Bang decided that Sweetie should be the first one to go inside the post office to start the job off by playing an innocent hostage, but none of us understood what the fuck she was saying but him, so we quickly changed his mind about that plan. The only thing that bitch could do right was drive and suck dick.

"This is the freaky geek, am I coming in clear?" Brain's voice came through our earpiece, making us crack up laughing.

"Yo, you loud and clear, homie," Pilla answered him.

"Alrighty then. Hello, ma'am, how are you today?" he spoke to the front desk clerk as we got in our jump-out positions, ready to take what we had come there for.

"Yo, boss man. The money orders are ready for pick up. Now!" Mikey shouted into the mic as he exited the post office's side door and sped walked down the alley. Pilla, Bang, and I jumped out the back of the van and entered the back door that our inside target had left open for us. Pilla and I ran to the storage room where we were told the money orders were stacked. I shot the door keypad with two bullets, and the door popped open. I threw the boxes to the floor as I searched for the packages we had come to get. When my brother walked up behind me, I could tell by the look on his face that this heist wasn't going to go as planned. He grabbed the manager, our inside target, tightly wrapped his muscular arm around his neck, and placed his ghost gun to his head.

"Yo, you playin' me? So, I get all the way here, and this nigga wants to play my crew!" he shouted. He drug the employee by his neck down the hallway to his office. I could hear my brother's angry voice booming through the door.

"Yo, boss man, we gotta get out of here, stat! The pig scanner says one is on the way, let's go!" Brains shouted through our earpieces. As soon as Pilla heard Mikey's voice, he ran down the hallway and darted out the back door we had come in. I darted to the office where my brother was with his hostage and kicked the door open. "Ay, bro, we gotta get out of here. Did you find the stash?" I asked him as I approached him from behind. I looked over at the employee who was now as white as a ghost, and he and I both knew this was the last day of his life. I walked to the side of the desk and grabbed the boxes of money orders and shoved them into my duffle bag.

"This nigga tried to play me. That's only six boxes; where are the ten you promised, you lying motherfucker?!" Bang screamed and continued to kick the man repeatedly.

"Ay, fuck it, this is fine for now. The pigs hot and near, let's go." I tugged at his arm. He brushed me off him, so I decided to exit the post office and head outside. On my way out, I heard two fatal gunshots as the victim screamed. I jumped in the van and held my head down. I knew what we were doing wasn't right, but neither was murdering innocent victims. I packed a gun, but I never used it. I gave my brother a sideways look when he hopped in the van and Sweetie sped off. I loved him, but I was ultimately disgusted with this nigga's greed. I could tell by the sinister smirk on that nigga's face that he was up to something. I knew my brother, and I was pretty sure he'd found the extra boxes of money orders that were missing. And I also knew that if he had, we would never know, because he would never tell it.

Thankfully, like many of our previous jobs, we escaped uncaptured and unharmed and were on our way back to Jersey.

♥

The last spot we hit had a nigga agged and stressed out, so I decided to hit a local bar near our hood. Most of the times when I went out, I did so alone. I was dressed down, wearing a simple Gucci screened t-shirt, jeans, and sneakers. I tied my waist-length, crinkly dreads up in a man bun that sat on the top of my head and hopped in my whip and made it downtown to Cheeks strip club. When I pulled my convertible Benz into the parking lot, I saw how thick the crowd was. I didn't want to mix and mingle with the crowd, I just wanted to enjoy a bottle or two of some strong cognac, while some fat-assed stripper made her ass clap in my face to make her rent money.

Big Dave, the bouncer who stood at the front door, motioned for me to come to the front of the line, and dapped me up when he spotted me. I only visited clubs on occasions, but here I was, always VIP. I walked over to the private section, took a seat, and watched the thirsty exotic dancers entertain every nigga in the club out of his paycheck. As soon as I sat down on the red leather couch that probably had remnants of ass munch juices, and random niggas' sperm left on it, the bartender walked over with an ice-cold bottle of Remy Martin OX. I nodded to her and thanked her before popping the top and filling my cup.

I rocked to the banging beat and gulped the liquid
numbness to enjoy my night.

"She Bad" by Cardi B and YG boomed through the
speakers as Khandi's fine ass clapped her ass in front of
me.

"Hey, boo, I haven't seen you in here in a while.
How have you been, daddy?" Khandi whispered in my ear
with her arms wrapped around my neck. "What's your
plans when you leave the club tonight?" I sat back from her
embrace and smiled. I knew what she wanted, and I was
probably going to give it to her, being that it had been a
couple months since a nigga fucked something.

"Shid, it's whatever, mami," I told her, placing my
large hands on her perfectly sculpted ass and squeezing it.
She placed a kiss on my cheek, then lifted me up from the
couch to follow her. My dick tingled in my jeans thinking
about the good-ass head I was about to receive. Khandi
could put Super Head out of business. This braud could
suck a golf ball through a garden hose. She swallowed the

dick with no hesitation, and she always caught every single drop of the mess she made and gulped it down her throat.

"Let me go get dressed and grab my bag. I'll meet you in the parking lot." I nodded and walked to the bar to close out my tab and head to my whip.

Before I could get out the exit door of the club, gunshots rang out, and bullets ricocheted off the stage mirrors, causing the crowd of partygoers to go wild. I jogged to my Jag and hopped in. I wanted a piece of Khandi's fat booty ass badly, but I wasn't risking my life for a piece of pussy. Fuck that shit, for real. I hopped on the interstate to make my way to the crib when my stomach started growling. I made a quick exit and headed down to Main Street to stop by Junior's bodega.

Junior's was a small mom and pop shop that served the best breakfast sandwiches on the east coast. Usually, the line of customers would be wrapped around the building, but I was glad I had made it early.

"What up, Junior? What time breakfast going to be ready?" I asked him after yawning and checking the time on my watch while taking a seat at the counter.

"In about fifteen minutes I'll be starting the grill up. You're early today, bub." He laughed while fixing a cup of coffee for an incoming customer. I always got the same thing: a bacon egg and cheese sandwich on sourdough bread, but I decided to look over the menu at items I hadn't tried.

"Hi, how are you? Can I put a to-go order in, please?" A woman came in and stood just a few feet away from me at the counter. After the cook told her he could assist her after gathering his food items from the back, she nodded, sat at the counter and started scrolling through her social media page on her phone.

I tried to keep my eyes to myself, but the way her grey, checkered, Kate Spade skirt tightly fit her curvaceous body had my soldier standing at attention. My eyes traveled from her plump thighs to her beautiful face. I couldn't forget her country, southern accent, or that fat ass pumpkin booty. This was my third time seeing shorty, and I wasn't letting her fine ass get away from me this time without at least getting her name and number. Fuck it, I was feeling confident today.

"How are you this morning, beautiful?" I asked her, then licked my lips, trying to ease my nervousness.

She looked around, then smiled, directing her light green eyes towards me, causing me to bite my lip.

"Who me?" she blushed, melting a nigga's heart. Damn, shorty was fine as fuck. I was glad she was so close to me this time. I could actually get a full look at her facial features. The cinnamon-brown freckles that lightly sprinkled her pudgy nose, her perfect white teeth, and her slightly caved dimple that graced her right cheek made me stare deeply into her gorgeousness.

I smiled at her and nodded. "I don't see anyone else around here, mami. You must not be from around here. Sounds like you have an accent?" I flirted with her a bit to open her up to me.

She laughed and nodded. "Well, I'm from Georgia. And where are you from, Mr. Asking-all-these-questions?" she giggled, turning me on even more. I could tell she was feeling me because the whole time we talked, she tried to avoid looking into my eyes.

"My name is Gw—Darren, and I'm from here." I smiled at her and extended my hand to shake hers.

She hesitated before accepting my gesture. "Here, as in Linden, or here as in Jersey?"

"Here as in the tri-state area. I'm from all around, but I was born in New York," I lied.

"So, Darren from here, what is there to do around here besides go to bars and clubs? I'm not really into that lifestyle."

Perfect, I thought. She was from out of state, fine, intelligent and classy. That was just the kind of woman I needed in my life. The geeks were always quiet freaks, and I couldn't wait to bring that side out of her.

"Well, there's a lot to do, Ms. Southern Boo—Beauty." I caught myself. "You just have to explore with the right person. I wouldn't mind showing you around. Maybe we can be friends?" I flirted with her.

"I wouldn't mind that. And by the way, I'm Shiri. Nice to meet you, Darren."

While Junior cooked our breakfast, we shared a brief conversation. She told me a little about where she was from and her career. My dick tingled in my designer jeans finding out that shorty was an accountant. There was something about numbers that turned a nigga on. I guess that was the one thing my brother and I shared.

"I usually take my breakfast to go, but I think I can spare a few moments to eat with my new friend." She smiled at me. I must admit, seeing the way Shiri scarfed down her homestyle skillet potatoes and grilled onions turned me on. I loved a woman who wasn't scared to eat because I had no problem feeding her fluffy ass. She was petite, fair skinned, and plump, just like I liked my women. I couldn't do shit with a skinny bitch. I loved cushion when I was pushing my inches deep inside her cream box.

We spent almost an hour just chilling over breakfast and chopping it up before we had to depart each other. When Junior placed our ticket on the table, I snatched it from Shiri and showed her the gentleman I was by picking up the tab. She tried to snatch it away from me, and that was when I had to let her know that she was dealing with a real nigga.

"Shorty, look, rule number one of our new friendship. When you're with me, you don't have to reach in your purse for anything but to refresh your lip gloss." I laughed, making her blush. "Hell, you don't even need your ID when you're spending time with a real man, shorty." She nodded and smiled.

"OK, so the selling cars business is treating you that good?" she asked, and almost made me spit out the hot coffee I was sipping. I had gotten so caught up with her beauty and conversation, I forgot I had told her that. I couldn't tell her the truth about being a thief and a crook. I had to at least get the pussy first.

"Yes, indeed it is, ma." I nodded and grabbed a napkin to wipe away the sweat beads that were forming on my forehead.

"Well, thanks for breakfast, new friend. Let me head down the street to start my shift for the day. It was nice meeting you." Shorty grabbed her to-go cup of coffee and excused herself before making her exit to start her long work day. She was elegant and classy as fuck. I could tell she was educated, too, by the way her graceful words flowed from her pleasantly plump lips. Since she wasn't from this area, that was a major plus.

I ordered a breakfast sandwich to go for Pop-Pop to drop off by Bang's and stared at her number saved in my phone, feeling proud of myself while I waited for my order.

I couldn't wait to show my new friend around.

♥Chapter Seven

BANG

I was really growing tired of this shit. I was praying that when I made it to the house, I could just rest without all the bitching from my shorty. A nigga was tired as fuck, and all I wanted to do was wash my nuts and hit the sack. Karissa and I had an on-again-off-again relationship for the past ten years. She had twin boys growing inside her uterus that made her a nagging bitch most of the time. I had love for my shorty, but she knew I wasn't ready to be a father right now, or probably ever in my life. I was a rough-around-the-edges thug. I was ruthless and uncontrollable, and Rissa knew that, but that didn't stop her ass from trying to make me change my life around on a daily. Then, on top of that, she never gave a nigga any pussy, and that was why I still had my bitches on the side. I understood she was almost eight months pregnant with twins, but when a nigga's dick got hard, her job as my woman was to make that nigga go soft again.

I sat in the recliner, put my feet up and grabbed the remote to turn on SportsCenter. I could feel my shorty's presence near, so I closed my eyes and tilted my head back, thinking maybe she would leave a nigga the fuck alone if she saw I was asleep.

THWAP!

Was this bitch serious right now? Rissa slapped the fuck out of me.

"Nigga, yo' ass ain't sleep. I'm tired of your shit, Aaron Thompson Sr.! I know you are messing around on me." She cried as tears welled up in her eyes. A nigga really didn't need this shit right about now. I'd had too much go on today to be dealing with her pregnancy hormones; those bitches stayed out of whack. "And I know you and Darren are doing more than just fixing cars down at that shop of yours. You haven't even been here all week to check on Pop-Pop. So, who is she? I'm listening!" she yelled, then folded her arms across our growing sons and sat on the footstool that was in front of me after slapping my feet off it.

I shook my head and blew air from my lips. I grabbed her petite hands and wrapped them around my neck.

"Now, baby, you know I don't want anyone but your big, pregnant ass. I know we can't make love like we usually do because of the pregnancy, so the only bitches I'm cheating on you with are Jergens and Palmisha." I stared at her and squinted my eyes, showing off my dimples, which made her blush every time she was mad at me.

"Yeah, whatever, nigga. I know you ain't just fucking yo' hand. But if and when I find out, I will cut your fucking dick off!" she screamed as she stomped up the steps. I was glad I had a meeting to go to tonight because I wasn't about to sit in this house and listen to her bitching when I couldn't fuck it out of her. I texted Sweetie to see if she was in the mood to swallow some dick.

♥

I was glad I had found the four extra boxes of money orders that nigga had tried to jib from me. I guess he wasn't happy with his cut, so he wanted to be greedy at the last minute, and it ended up costing him his fucking life. After seeing my parents murdered in cold blood at a very young age, I didn't give a fuck about anyone's life anymore, not even my own. It was sad but true.

We had one more job to hit this year, and that would set me up so my lady and our babies would be straight for life, and I could pay this bitch off who had been hounding me since she found out my secret. I pulled out the extra money orders I had hidden in my jacket on our last heist and began to stash them in the ceiling when I was interrupted by a knock on my office door. I quickly closed the opening I'd made in the ceiling and replaced the ladder in the corner before opening it. Surprisingly, Pilla was waiting for me on the other side. I let him in and told him to grab a seat. He gave me a dirty look, shook his head and said he would rather stand up. I didn't know what was eating this nigga, but I wasn't in the mood for his daily bitching today. I could tell he was bothered by something by the look of worry written on his face.

"What's up Pilla the Killa?" I broke the ice by trying to get him to open up about whatever he was worried about.

"Yo, B, I-I need a favor, homie. A big favor. Just until the next job, and you can keep my cut of the pay—"

He halted his words when I gave him a sideways look and brushed his hand across his waves.

"It's my mom's. Man, sh-she…" He paused, brushed his hand down his face and looked towards the ceiling before continuing to beg me for a favor. Since I'd met Pilla a couple years back, he was always asking to borrow money. He was a frivolous spender; he blew all his bands on butt naked hoes down at Cheeks. I was tired of fronting that nigga money he could never pay back. I was aware of his mother's lung cancer, but he'd asked for money before to help pay his mother's medical bills, but this nigga still tricked off to random hoes at different clubs nightly. I didn't have my mother anymore, so, honestly, I didn't give one fuck about his. It wouldn't bring my mom's back. I stood and shook my head before passing by him and heading towards my office door.

"I'm all out of favors, homie." I shrugged and left him standing in the doorway. I had a good hour before I had to be back home, dealing with my pregnant bitch, and after I paid my crew their percentages, I would have just enough time for my li'l dip to swallow my inches down her moist throat before going back home.

♥Chapter Eight

SHIRI

I exhaled deeply and rolled my eyes as I refreshed my lip gloss in Khodi's mirror. She had planned for us to go on a double date tonight with one of her many boo thangs and his cousin and, at first, I wasn't down with it at all. The doorman buzzed to let us know the guys had arrived downstairs. After checking each other's outfits and making sure our makeup was on point, and there wasn't any lipstick on our teeth, we headed out the door to the elevator. My phone chimed from an incoming text from Mr. Sexual Chocolate. I was glad I had met him down at Jimmy's bodega that day. Darren was an absolute gentleman. He had a tough guy swag I loved, and when I was with him, I felt so safe and secure as if I had no worries in the world.

Darren: So, what's up? What's your plans for tonight beautiful?

Me: Just going to a business dinner meeting with my best friend, what's up? What you got going on tonight?

Even though Darren and I had been talking on the phone for a couple of weeks, we still hadn't gone out on an official date yet. He seemed to always be busy with his sickly grandfather or his business. We stayed in contact, though. Most of the time when we talked, our conversations pertained to my job. I continued to date other men because I didn't know exactly what his intentions were with me just yet. But, deep down inside, I hoped we could hit it off one day, or at least be cutty buddies. A sister was feening for some. It had been too long, and my poor vibrator had died on me completely after trying to revive it with new batteries three times.

"Oh, come on, Ri. Jared is nice, and he's been trying to get at you for a while now. Just give him a chance, OK?" Khodi persuaded me as she stood behind me, fluffing my curls.

"OK, girl, but this is the last date I'm going on with you choosing for me. These east coast niggas are not used to a woman like me. It's just probably not meant for me to find a man out here." I shrugged, then grabbed my clutch and walked towards the front door so we could meet Kendrick and his friend Jared downstairs in the foyer.

****

I sat across from Jared in the restaurant, picking at my plate with a fork in my right hand as my left elbow rested on the table. My date Jared was still rambling about sports and, honestly, I wasn't interested. Khodi kicked me underneath the table and gave me a 'what's wrong' look. I grabbed my phone and purse and excused myself to the ladies' room, and that was her cue to join me.

I quickly ran into the bathroom stall to relieve myself from the three glasses of wine I had drunk earlier that helped me tune out my self-absorbed date. I wasn't sure why Khodisha had hooked me up with a man like him. Jared was attractive, though, standing over six feet tall. He had smooth, caramel-colored skin, and light-brown hazel eyes that complemented his straight white teeth, but I could tell he was a jock at first glance. His chiseled body was perfectly toned, and the silly, soft pink shirt he wore to dinner appeared to be two sizes too small. On top of that, he hadn't stopped talking about himself or his many years of playing football the whole time at dinner. My bestie knew me, and she knew I was easily annoyed by a nigga like him, so I was ready to go.

"Ri! Where are you, boo?" Khodi called from outside the stall as I finished my business and wiped myself before exiting the stall.

"Girl, I had to piss so bad, shit!" I joined her at the sink to wash my hands.

"So, what do you think of Jared?"

I grabbed the paper towel and dried my hands before picking up my phone and scrolling to an incoming text message from my new boo.

"Do you really wanna know what I think about that self-absorbed jackass? He hasn't stopped self-loathing since our entrees arrived." I smacked my lips at her and rolled my eyes.

"Well, big egos are accompanied by a big dick, most of the time!" She looked at me and pretended to hump the air.

Darren: What's up shorty? You ignoring a nigga now? How's your date going?

I laughed to myself before texting him back.

Me: Who said I was on a date? If you don't believe me, here's the address. Come pick me up.

I sent my location to him and told Khodi I would meet them at the table. As soon as she left the restroom, I snuck out of the restaurant and walked to the back of the parking lot. He told me he was only fifteen minutes away, so I didn't mind waiting. When Darren pulled up in a candy red Lamborghini, I was shocked. He had told me the car sales business was treating him right. He lifted the door for me, and I slid in right as Khodi was running outside to see where I had disappeared to.

"See ya later, best friend!" I shouted to Khodi as Darren whipped down the freeway.

I know you're with him but you're callin' me

I turned the knob up on the radio as "Love and Hennessy" boomed through his speakers.

I started to feel the beat and rocked to it.

"Aye, Mami, you better be lucky this your first time in my ride because I don't let anyone touch my radio, boo," he laughed.

I playfully rolled my eyes at him. "Whatever. So, where are you off to on this Saturday night?" I asked, turning down the music, then holding my hands up in surrender when he gave me the side-eye.

"Well, I was just running a couple errands and getting payroll straight for my workers, that's all. How was your date, ma?"

I looked at him and tried to fight a smile from escaping my lips.

"Yo, I told you before, ma. You ain't gotta lie to me about nothing. Be honest with me, and I'll return the favor. We're not in a relationship yet, so you good with me, love. I know that nigga wasn't too much of shit because you called a real nigga to come scoop you."

All I could do was laugh. It was so funny to me how men wanted to know our every move, but we had to try and figure them out. I decided to ignore his statement and sit back and enjoy the ride. Any other woman would've been skeptical about being swept up by a man they had just met, who was driving them to an unknown destination, but I felt so secure when I was with Darren. He made me comfortable, and when I was with him, nothing else in the world mattered but us. I rested my head on the red leather headrest and enjoyed the music on the forty-five-minute ride to our destination.

After putting a passcode in on a keypad at a large bronze gate, Darren pulled into a garage of a high-rise that was near the ocean. I sat up in my seat as my eyes grew wide, taking in the beautiful surroundings. He parked in between a Range Rover and convertible Mercedes Benz, then hopped out and waited for me on the passenger side with an extended hand.

"Where are we?" I asked, looking around and tucking a loose strand of hair behind my ear.

"This is my place. We're going up to get dressed for our date night." He smiled at me as he guided me through the dimly lit garage, holding my hand.

"But I-I didn't bring any change of clothes," I told him as he pressed the floor-level button on the elevator's keypad.

"You really don't listen to me, huh, shorty? I told you when I met you that when you're with me, you don't need a damn thing. And I meant that." He licked his plump lips and squinted his eyes as the doors opened, revealing his luxurious bachelor pad. He grabbed my hand again, and I followed him into the living room. I looked around and admired the ultra-black modern leather sectional that sat on top of an exquisite black and gold carpet. The walls of his living room were aligned with the best autograph pieces from Picasso, and with the touch of a button, the two-way shades slid open, revealing the beautiful waves that the moonlight shone from.

"Wow, this is beautiful! Are we still in Jersey?" I laughed.

He came up behind me, wrapping his arms around my waist after handing me a glass of Moscato.

The elevator chimed, which made him let go of me and walk to it to welcome his visitor.

"Bonjour misère!" A woman greeted him as she glided on the custom mosaic tile with her two male assistants, who looked like twin brothers, following closely behind her. They each came in with rolling suitcases in their hands and walked straight to me. One of the assistants outstretched my arms in the air, then began taking measurements of my body while the other played in my hair. "I think we should do a sequin V-neck with an updo for Ms. Lady." The one who played in my hair spoke to the other assistant, who nodded in agreeance.

"Here you go, Madame. Now off to salle de bains to freshen up a bit, oui?"

I nodded and began walking to the bathroom to take a quick shower before getting pampered by the dream team Darren had ordered. I was definitely going to enjoy this. I'd never been treated like a princess before by anyone but my father, so to find a man who knew how to cater to a woman was remarkable.

After my shower, I returned to the living room in my robe and sat in the chair, and the man started on my hair while the other did my makeup. I picked up my phone when it chimed from an incoming text from Darren, who I had noticed was no longer in the room.

Darren: I'll let you ladies have that floor. I'm downstairs getting dressed. When you're done, meet me in the garage. OK, boo?

Me: Sure love.

I did a once-over in the floor-length mirror and was filled with glee. The twins had beat my face to the gods in heaven, my shoulder length hair was now pinned up in wand curls, and the red sequin crisscrossed dress hugged my body and accentuated every one of my bodacious curves. I couldn't wait to see what my new friend had in store for us tonight.

The glam crew gathered their belongings and followed me into the elevator, then we headed down to the parking garage. When we arrived, they said their goodbyes, and I walked up to Darren, who stood with his back against a navy-blue, silver-topped Bentley limousine. He was dressed down in a black Versace tuxedo, but his jacket was off, his tie wasn't tied, and his sleeves were rolled up. He had my kitty tingling in my G-string. He held a double bouquet of white long-stemmed roses in his hands. His eyes grew wide as I slowly walked to him, strutting in my nude Red Bottoms. The way he sucked in his bottom lipped turned me on even more. He pulled me to him by my waist and immediately placed his lips over mine. I leaned back from his embrace and looked deeply into his doe-shaped eyes. He smelled so good, and the way his long dreadlocks were braided back in two ponytails turned me on even more. If we didn't get going to our destination, I would take his chocolate ass upstairs and show him some real southern lovin'.

He opened the door for me, and I sat on the seat as he slid in behind me, wrapping his arms around my waist again, and passing me the bouquet of flowers.

"Thanks, D. This is so nice of you. Thanks for everything. The clothes and being pampered. You really know how to take care of a woman, don't you? Too bad you're single." I laughed, watching him slide to the mini bar and pour himself a shot of Hennessy on the rocks.

"Well, you deserve it, boo. I first want to apologize for taking so long to take you out as I promised. It's just that business has been kinda busy lately. But I've enjoyed our conversations over the past few weeks. You're definitely different from the women out here."

"Well, I'm glad we're here now. So, where are we going tonight? You have us dressed so fancy."

He took the double shot of Hennessy to his head and filled his glass up again. "You said you've never been to Atlantic City, right? So, that's where we're going for the weekend."

"The weekend? So, you're just going to kidnap me, huh?"

"If that's what you want to call it. I'm just trying to make up for lost time. But if you don't want to stay, I can have my driver take you back to your car. You don't have to do nothing you don't want to do, shorty." I nodded and sat back in my seat, then grabbed his hand and intertwined our fingers, placing them on my lap.

"I'm good, and I'm ready for our weekend getaway. I know you would never let anything happen to me, baby." I looked him in his eyes, and seconds later, our tongues were wrestling in each other's mouths.

Detective Marissa Benson

I sat on the edge of the table in the big meeting room and shook my head as I read over the paperwork in my hands. I grabbed the remote again and pressed play on the video I had watched moments earlier. I studied the body movement of the armed robbers as they ransacked the Florida post office. My captain said I was reaching, being that this wasn't my case, but I believed the spots that had been targeted lately were the handiwork of the same crew.

I wasn't exactly sure where the crew was from, but after viewing footage from the last few heists, the body movements of the suspects looked highly familiar. I noticed there was never more than three suspects of the crew at a time during their planned robberies.

I zoomed the camera in closer and studied the hand tattoo of the suspect who instantly executed our victim. I knew I had seen that tattoo before. I heard voices coming near the meeting room, so I grabbed the remote and shut the TV off, then grabbed the stack of files and buried them at the bottom of the coffee cabinet. I felt a great deal of achievement knowing I had an idea of the identity of these suspects. They had gotten away with many heists, but I guaranteed this was the last one, and I was going to make sure of it.

♥Chapter Nine

PILLA

I stood over my mother Mary's hospital bed in her room, fighting back the tears that wanted to escape my weary eyes. Just two years ago, my mother was diagnosed with lung cancer. My mother had always been a strong woman. She was a registered nurse, and even though she was sick, she still worked her ass off to provide for me and my four younger brothers and sisters. She held down the fort without any help from our absent fathers, and she was the true definition of a single mother. My mother was also stubborn like me, so I didn't find out about her sickness until eight months ago. She was on her last night shift at the local hospital downtown when she was rushed to the emergency wing, and that was when I found out she had lung cancer. Shortly after that, it spread to her spine.

I spent a lot of my time down at the strip club, letting expensive cognac numb the aching pain that filled my heart every time I thought about my mother's condition.

Bang thought I fucked off all my money at the strip club, but that wasn't the case. Since my mother's condition had gotten worse, I was taking care of my siblings and whatever her insurance didn't cover for her hospital bills.

I took a seat next to her bed and picked up the clipboard that her nurse had brought in earlier. I exhaled deeply as my eyes scanned over her monthly charges. I blankly stared at the total amount that was overdue. I shook my head and brushed my hands down my face. I hated Bang's bitch ass now more than ever. He was so fucking selfish and greedy, and I wasn't the only member in the crew who was growing tired of his selfishness. My mind quickly drifted off to the first day I met him, years ago.

I grew up in Brooklyn, New York. Being the oldest of many kids caused me to drop out of high school in the ninth grade. From the time I was fourteen years old, until the time I met up with my new crew, I was a lookout and errand boy for one of the biggest kingpins in Brooklyn named Billy Boy.

Working under Billy Boy was cool, but he didn't pay me that well because I refused to graduate from only being the lookout boy to pushing weight for him. I knew the consequences of me choosing that lifestyle, and I knew I couldn't leave my siblings or our mother out here hopeless if I ended up dead or in jail.

One day, I was working down at Jimmy's Bodega for Billy Boy, and all hell broke loose. I was posted inside, playing Pac-Man on one of the game machines, when a young, hooded thug, who was wearing a ski mask, came through the door waving a loaded gun in the air, begging the storekeeper to empty the safe.

What the young thug didn't know was that Jimmy might have been an elderly Puerto-Rican man, but he stayed packing. As soon as the thug demanded money from him by placing the barrel of his .357 to his temple, Jimmy's son came from the back of the store and lit the robber's ass up.

Later on, we found out that what the young gangster had come into the store for wasn't money. He had come in to jack the stash of bricks Billy Boy had hidden behind Jimmy's register. My mouth dried up as I saw the young man's soul leave his body as he hit the cold, tile floor.

"Look, you ain't seen nothing, and you don't know nothing!" Jimmy shouted at me, grabbing my shirt collar. I frighteningly nodded and stood, preparing to catch the next train that was headed back to Brooklyn. I ran towards the back door, then halted when I saw the brand-new pair of Jordan 12 that were on the now-deceased teen's feet. I looked around to make sure Jimmy and his son were out of sight before I snatched the pair of shoes from his feet and skidded down the alley. I tucked the shoes into the front pocket of my hoodie and ran down the alley until I tripped at the corner of the alley and fell smack dab on my face, cutting it open.

"Fuck!" I screamed while trying to stand. I was helped up by a light-skinned nigga who looked like he was Puerto Rican or some shit.

"Aye, homie, you work for Billy Boy, right?" I gave him a confused look and shook my head, then started walking away. "If you looking for a better job making some real money, I might have something for you." I stopped in my tracks and turned back to hear him out. He laced me up on him and his brother's business and told me what I needed to do to join their crew. And from that day forth, I was recruited to Stack Gang.

My mother's coughing snapped me out of my thoughts. "Kendrick is that you, baby?" her soft voice cracked. I stood so she could see my face.

"Yeah, it's me, mama. How are you feeling?" I asked, trying to hide my emotions as she motioned for me to give her a sip from the plastic cup of ice water that sat at her bedside.

I grabbed the cup and held the straw gently to her lips, quenching her thirst.

"I'm-I'm gon' be all right, Kenny. You just take care of my babies. And did my nurse give you the paperwork for the hospital bills? I don't know how long they're going to keep me this time because the insurance is only going to pay for so much—"

"Mommy don't worry about any of that. I got everything taken care of." I placed a soft kiss on her forehead to ease her worries." She started to mouth something, then sleep consumed her body from the pain meds her nurse had administered to her earlier when I had first come in.

My emotions were overpowering me, so I decided to leave the hospital for the night after I called my mother's sister to come in and sit with her until I got back the next morning. I jumped in my whip and hopped on the freeway as my mind drifted back to the day I asked Bang for another loan. That nigga was so fucking selfish, it was ridiculous. He didn't give a fuck about anyone but himself. That shit was going to catch up with his ass one day, and one day soon.

My cell chimed from an incoming text from my li'l shorty, Khodi. I had been fucking her off and on for almost eight months now, and we were starting to get serious. Even though I cared for mami deeply in my heart, I would never reveal the truth about me to her. I catered to her and always took her to expensive restaurants and out on shopping dates, but she didn't know I was just another thug-ass nigga from the BK who was trying to make it in this world. When I didn't answer her text message, she called me.

I wanted to ignore the call but decided against it. "What's up, boo?"

"Hey, Zaddy," she cooed into my ear, almost making my dick rise. "Are we still on for dinner and drinks tonight?" she asked.

"Yeah, I'm leaving from Mommy now, and on my way to you."

"OK, I'm getting dressed now. I'll be ready when you get here, babe," she promised before we ended our phone call.

I quickly did a U-turn on the freeway and made my way to Linden, New Jersey, where we would hold our meetings before our heists. Ever since the day of our last payout, when I went in to chop it up with Bang, some shit had been on my mind. I noticed he had been acting shady since the Cali job. Well, that nigga was always funny acting, but I could read the hell out of people, and that day, that nigga had that Obama look on his face like he knew some shit he couldn't tell us. I also noticed how one of his ceiling tiles was loose over his desk.

Finding out the clerk had lied to him about the promised amount of money orders we were scheduled to pick up had put us all in a bind. The amount we would've received from that one job would have been enough for me to cover all of my mother's hospital bills and set my siblings' college funds up for life.

I pulled down Main Street behind a large van and peeped the scene out before making my next move. I stared at Thompson's Garage, which was our cover up for our business, making sure there was no traffic coming in or out of the building. Reaching in the back seat of my car, I slid an all-black hoodie over my head and jumped out my whip, securing my banger on the right side of my waist.

With the handle of my gun, I broke the padlock that kept the steel gate chained and used the barrel of my gun to break the glass door. I knew Bang kept an alarm on the spot, so I knew I had to be quick as fuck not to get caught. I darted down the hallway, making my way to the office, and kicked the door open.

I used the mini flashlight that was in the pocket of my hoodie to look around the small office for something to step on to get closer to the ceiling. I quickly found a ladder behind a file cabinet and placed it near the loose tile I had seen that day. My adrenaline rose, and sweat beads covered my forehead and the back of my neck as I gently pushed the tile up from the ceiling. I stuck my head inside the hole in the ceiling and looked around with my light. I spotted the same black duffle bag Bang had across his chest on our Cali job. I pulled the straps of the bag closer to me, and that was when it fell through the hole in the ceiling, and to the floor, revealing what I'd felt all along when the money orders sprinkled over the floor like confetti.

I scraped up what I could and threw them inside the bag before running down the hallway to make my exit, bumping into a tall figure along the way. "Pill? Is that you? What are you doing in here?"

I stopped in my tracks and slowly turned around, meeting Mikey's face. "Brains! What's up, homie?" I nervously greeted him, trying to brush off my visual nervousness.

He had an awkward look on his face as he looked me up and down, stopping at the black duffle bag I held in my hands. "Well, Boss Man called me to come by and check things out when he got an alert that the alarm went off, but I can see—" He stopped talking and placed his hands on his forehead. "Wait a minute, are you breaking in here?" he asked with wide eyes. He pulled out his cell and started scrolling his call log. I pulled my heater from my waist and placed it in the middle of his forehead.

"Don't do it, Brains. Now, look, I can tell you exactly what I was doing here, but first, what I need you to do is go over to that keypad and turn off the alarm, and I'll hold this for you," I threatened, snatching his cell phone from his hands. I swallowed the large lump in my throat as I impatiently waited for him to do as I asked.

"Your greedy ass boss was holding out on us, homie!" I shouted, not lowering my pistol from in front of his face as he stood with his hands surrendered in the air. "Remember the post office job?" he nodded, giving me a confused look. "Well, look what I found. He's been stashing it away from us." I kept my gun pointed at him with my right hand and unzipped the duffle bag I carried across my shoulder with my left, pulling out the evidence of hidden money orders I had found before I was interrupted by Steven Q. Urkel.

"Look—" he stuttered. "Can you put the fucking gun down, homie? You don't have to kill me. I'm a geek, not a snitch," he laughed, making a grin spread across my face. I sucked my teeth and shook my head. Mikey's ass was always so goofy in every situation; he was only serious when it came down to crunching numbers with jobs.

"OK, look, we are going to have to get out of here because I'm sure Bang or Gwop will be showing up, especially since I haven't answered his phone calls since you're holding my phone hostage," he snickered. I passed him back his ringing cell.

"Aye, boss. Yeah, I made it here. It seems like someone tried to break in, but the spot was empty when I got here. I'm still looking around, but I don't see anything that's missing. OK, cool. I'll be waiting for you when you get here. One."

I squinted my eyes, egging Brains to let me in on what Bang had said during their phone call. "You might wanna leave. He said he's on his way and will be here in about forty-five minutes. I'll meet you at your car."

I nodded and exited the building after sticking my gun in the back of my pants. About five minutes later, Mikey brought his nerdy ass out the back of the building, and I flicked my headlights to show him where I was parked. Even though I had just gotten caught stealing from my probably soon-to-be ex-boss, I had no doubts about trusting Brains. If you couldn't trust Brains, you couldn't trust anybody.

He gave me a head nod and briskly walked over to my car and slid into the passenger seat. "Now, what's up, Kendrick?" he smirked, using my government name. "What's all this for? And you gotta talk fast because Bang said he's on his way."

I exhaled before speaking. "After the last job, I went to Bang, asking him if he could help me out with a loan until the next job for my mother's hospital bills. He told me he was all out of favors. I noticed something funny with the ceiling that day I was in his office speaking with him, so I decided to come back and inspect my suspicions—"

"Inspect your suspicions, huh?" he mimicked, laughing.

"Man, this is some real fucked-up shit, though. I can't believe he would do something like this to us after all we've done for him." I could tell he was upset internally because Mikey was brown-skinned, and his face instantly turned beet red. This was my first time seeing him upset since I'd known him.

"Look, I can give you half of what's in this bag if you keep this between us." I persuaded him to keep my secret.

"OK, that's cool. You're secret is safe with me. Truth is, I'm starting to get tired of doing these heists. I mean, the money is good, but I'm still young and have my whole life ahead of me. I should be in college, going to school for accounting or something, not doing this illegal shit." He let out a nerdy giggle before hopping out my whip.

"Aye, get gone before that nigga gets here, bro." He dapped me up before jogging across the street as I sped off into the night.

♥

Ring! Ring!

"Yes, my love?" I sang into the phone, not checking the caller ID.

"Kendrick!" Brains screeched into my ear, catching me off guard as I pulled into a nearby gas station and hopped out.

"What's going on, nigga? You just scared the hell out of me. I thought you were my shorty." I hopped out of my car and walked inside to purchase a box of condoms. I had a lot of built-up stress, and I knew Khodi was going to be ready to fuck it up out a nigga.

"Hey, I put the ceiling tile back. I know Bang, and he's a sneaky motherfucker. He will spaz the fuck out if he walks in here and sees that shit right off hand. I'll let him find out about that shit without me."

He laughed into the phone before ending our call. I grabbed my box from the counter and walked out of the store, accidentally bumping into Bang, which caused me to almost lose my breath.

"What's wrong, nigga? You act like you just saw a fucking ghost or some shit." He smacked his lips and looked me up and down before walking into the store. Secretly, I was growing tired of this nigga. He was rude as fuck and selfish, and that was the reason most of the crew despised him.

I paid the attendant a small tip for filling my tank and hopped in my whip to head to my baby.

♥

"Ahhh! Mmmnn! Yes, baby!" Khodi screamed as she rode my dick backward. I had a lot of frustration built up inside me, so I was sure I was going to break her back and bed tonight. We were currently on round three of our sex match when Khodi finally tapped out after reaching her fifth climax. She had the best pussy I'd ever fucked, but shorty was wearing me out tonight. She slowly lifted her creamy pussy off my numb, defeated dick.

I exhaled deeply as I watched her beautiful, dark-chocolate body sashay to her bedroom door to grab her silky, pink robe and slide it on. I was starting to love shorty a little bit, and I knew, sooner or later, I would have to reveal the truth about my lifestyle. I just didn't want her to stop fucking with a nigga when she found out about the real me.

"I'm thirsty as fuck, bae! You want some water?" my black beauty asked as she headed to exit the bedroom. I nodded.

"Meet me in the shower, boo." She smiled and agreed as I hopped up and walked into her attached bathroom to wash our sex juices from my body. As the steamy water sprinkled over my skin, my head filled with thoughts of my busy day. From my mother to the secret I'd found out Bang was hiding, a nigga was hurt and felt disrespected more than anything. Motherfuckers were so ready to be a leader but didn't know how to lead. He was a selfish-ass nigga, and I was going to make sure he got what was coming to him.

I pulled back the shower curtain and yelled to Khodi, "Yo, what's taking so long? All the hot water gon' be out before you get in with me, babe."

"I'm coming and bringing your phone. Someone is calling!" she yelled back.

I turned the knob to shut off the shower and pulled the curtain back. Khodi stood there with a disgusted look on her face and my cell phone in her hand. I stepped out of the tub and grabbed my ringing cell that showed my aunt's number, flashing across the screen. I hurriedly answered, hoping she had good news about my mother's condition. I placed the phone on my ear and wrapped a large bath towel around my waist while I waited for her to answer my call. I sat on the bed, still wondering why shorty had a messed-up look on her face. She paced back and forth in front of me, not saying a word.

"What's this?" Khodi asked, holding a stack of money orders in her hands as my aunt answered the phone weeping, telling me my mother had now been freed from her pain and misery.

SHIRI

"Oh, my goodness, Darren, this is so beautiful." I looked around the blanket he'd laid out for our picnic under the stars in the park. I had to go home soon for my mother's birthday, but I was going to miss waking up to my man daily. Since our first date, Darren and I had been inseparable. On the days I was off, and he wasn't tied up with his car business, we spent time together. He'd kept his word and showed me around the east coast. Almost every other night, we were visiting exquisite museums or fancy restaurants.

We had just left the poetry slam in Brooklyn, and now we were enjoying a nice candlelit dinner under the stars. I had to show my new man that a sister could burn, and besides, I was tired of eating pizza and subs all the time. I was from the south, so I whipped up some southern fried chicken with garlic mash potatoes, sweet buttered corn, and cornbread. I loaded up a plate with the savory goodness and passed it to him. I must admit, I loved the way he smacked and licked his fingers as he inhaled the food from his plate without breathing. "Slow down, bae," I laughed.

"Girl, I thought you was playing when you said you could burn. Yo, I ain't had no good food like this since my mom's was here."

I crawled over to my man, rubbed my hands through his dreads and massaged his scalp. He pulled me down to his lap, straddling my legs on top of his. "I'm going to miss you, babe," I told him, looking into his dark-brown eyes before pecking his lips.

"Nah, shorty. You ain't gon' be thinking about me, yo. You going to be doing there with your Atlanta boyfriend and not have me on your mind."

"Oh, yeah? Well, if all these people wasn't here in the park, I would show you just how much I'ma miss you."

"Shit, Mami, let's wrap up this chicken and take it to the crib then.

Chapter Ten

GWOP

Southern Booty: I miss you so much bae. When are you coming back in town?

Me: Soon baby. Just let me finish handling this business first. I miss you too. It won't be much longer, I promise.

Southern Booty: OK. Be safe, I love you.

Me: Love you back Shorty.

Inside, a nigga was smiling wide like the Kool-Aid man. I couldn't believe Mami had just texted that she loved me. I said it back because, truthfully, I felt the same way about Shiri. She was different, nothing like these money hungry ass east coast brauds, and that was the reason I spoiled the fuck out of her bougie ass. I wouldn't mind putting a ring on her finger one day and changing her last name to Thompson. The family thing would have to wait, though. I wasn't sure I was ready to start a family just yet, but we had plenty of time for all that. I couldn't wait to get back home to my baby so I could dick her down. The way her juicy pussy squirted on my thick shaft every time we made love had a nigga sprung, I couldn't even lie.

I wasn't going to lie; a nigga was falling hard for shorty. I couldn't wait until we got back home so I could be booed up with my li'l baby. I wanted so badly to tell her the truth about me and my profession, but I didn't want to scare her off. I knew that sooner or later; I would have to either come clean or break up with her.

I was tired of my brother controlling my life. He felt I couldn't have a bitch, but he had one he went home to every night and a bitch on the side. Pussy had never changed my mind about getting money, but with Ri, it was more than just sex. For the first time in a nigga's life, I felt like I was in love, real love. Even though I wasn't myself, I could be myself with her. She made me want to explore things in this life other than hood shit. Who knows, maybe down the line my shorty and I could have a li'l shorty or two. I sat back and thought about how she looked in that banging-ass Versace dress she wore to Atlantic City that night I took her out. I could only imagine how beautiful she would look in a custom-made Vera Wang bridal gown.

I could tell my brother was agitated about something by his ill-ass attitude.

I looked over to my right and saw the evil scowl Bang had on his face as he loaded the clip of his AK-47.

"You lost something, nigga?" I asked, then cracked up laughing to ease the tension that Brains could clearly see we shared at the moment.

"Fuck you, bruh." He sucked his teeth and laughed back at me nonchalantly. I didn't know what was eating this nigga, but he'd had a fucked-up attitude ever since he and Pilla got into it after the last job. He was tripping for nothing if you asked me, because with Pilla gone, that meant we only had to split the money five ways now. I'd always had a funny feeling about Pilla's ass since the first day I'd met him. He was from Brooklyn, and those BK niggas moved real grimy. He knew not to cross me though because I would bury a bullet in his fucking dome with no hesitation. I didn't exactly know what was up between him and my brother that made them get into it that day, and knowing my brother, he wasn't going to let me know either.

We finally arrived at our next job, a Walmart Supercenter in Kenner, Louisiana. It was a Friday afternoon in the middle of Mardi Gras season, and the great state of Louisiana was packed with tourists from all across the world who were ready and willing to show their perky boobs on girls gone wild for some random, horny pervert to hurl a loop of plastic beads at their drunk asses. Our inside connect was a soon-to-be single mother, who was a bank teller at the bank located inside the store. She had formed an undercover drug habit that caused her to fail a piss test. Her ex-husband had called the Department of Family Services on her when their young daughter was burned by a curling iron while she was in the next room, snorting a couple lines of coke. It was a sad situation, but the unfit bitch needed her portion of the 550,000 dollars to help pay for a lawyer so she could gain custody of her young daughter again.

I told myself this would be my last heist. After this large amount, I would be set with the rest of the money I had saved. Maybe then my Southern Booty and I could run away and start a new life far away, where no one knew us, and be happy. Sweetie pulled the get-away ride on the side of the shopping center that was just across the parking lot from our hit.

"Aye, boss." Brains chirped in our ear. "We have a li'l situation…"

Sweetie turned around and faced my brother with a look of worry on her face as she pulled her black Chanel shades from her made-up face.

Bang angrily exhaled before speaking. "What's up, Mikey? Talk to me, Brains, what's going on?" he said with a voice full of concern as he shook his head from side to side.

"The target says the truck is running fifteen minutes behind schedule. Something about a five-car pileup down the road, so they will be pulling up in another twenty minutes."

"Fuck!" Bang shouted. My palms grew sweaty with anticipation. Since we'd left home, I had a gut feeling something wasn't going to go right, and I learned as a young boy from my Pop-Pop that you always follow your first mind. I looked over at my brother, then blew air from my lips and put my head down.

"Bang, we can still pull this off. According to my calculations—"

"Aye, Mr. Smarty Pants, spare me the scientific calculations and just simplify it for me, please." Bang laughed to ease both of our anxiousness.

"No prob, Bob. Hi, excuse me, could you by chance tell me which aisle the Trojans, sensitive lubricated condoms are located on?" he spoke to a Walmart employee as he pretended to walk around the store as a shopping customer.

"Brains, you know good and well you ain't getting no got damn pussy!" I shouted into my mic, making my brother and Sweetie crack up laughing.

"I gets plenty of pussy. The honeys love a big dick smart nigga. I can teach them a thang or two while I lay the pipe!" he burst out laughing.

"OK, our target, Ms. Scratch and Sniff, says the usual armored truck drivers, Jimmy and David, are scheduled to pick up the deposit today. She also said Jimmy is an older gentleman who kind of has a bladder problem—"

"Come on, Papi, get to it!" Sweetie intervened, making Brains aka Sir Talk-a-Lot explaining his plan for the delayed job.

"So, bing, bang, boom, when David brings the deposit back to the truck and loads it up, and Jimmy hops out to drain the main vein, that's when we take action. Capiche?"

"Sounds like a plan to me," Bang added.

I nodded to my brother, secured my heater in my waist, slid my cell into my pants pocket and placed my black ski mask on top of my head.

♥

"All right, bay-bee, we got some action, Papi," Sweetie sang in her thick accent. I lifted my head and sat in a squatted position. I pulled my ski mask over my head and held my pistol tight in my hand. I was ready to get this shit over with, so I could go back to Jersey and lay up with my boo.

Within minutes, the armored truck pulled into their usual parking spot in front of the busy store. Bang gave the signal to Mikey to let him know that the pick-up officer was on his way in. The younger officer exited the passenger side of the truck and walked inside the store with his collection bag. The older armored officer sat in the driver's seat with his phone wedged in between his ear and shoulder while he ran his mouth and shoved a triple bacon Rally's cheeseburger down his throat, followed by a big gulp. I shook my head. These some sloppy-ass niggas, but more careless they were, the easier it made our job.

According to Brains' scientific calculations, we had just about eight minutes left before the two officers switched positions. My heart thumped hard inside my chest as I stayed in position, ready to pounce on these niggas as soon as Sweetie gave us our cue.

"Now, Papi!" she screamed as the officer with the money bag exited the store. These niggas were real sloppy. One officer was to always stay put in the driver's seat while the other was out of the truck, but Old Man Jimmy the piss-master couldn't hold his bladder. As soon as he saw his partner exiting the store, he jumped out of the truck and made his way to the front door. My brother slid the van's back door open, and we rolled out as our gofer disappeared into the busy traffic.

Like clockwork, we ran up to David and attempted to snatch the money from him, but he had a death grip on the bags. He tried reaching for his pistol, and that was when Bang shot him in the leg.

"Oh, no! I hear gunshots! I'm on my way back to you guys," Sweetie cried in my earpiece. I could hear the tires screeching in the parking lot as she pulled back up. Everything happened so fast, I didn't even notice my brother was nowhere in sight.

"I got the bags, boss," Brains' voice boomed in my earpiece.

"Go ahead! I'll catch up with y'all. I'm fine," Bang chimed in. I jumped into the getaway van and slammed the door shut as Mikey hopped in behind me.

"Fuck!" I shouted as I noticed the armored truck officers were following close on our tail. These niggas were sloppy, but they didn't want to lose their job today.

"Sweetie!" I yelled. "Go, go, go!" I loaded my AK-47 and cracked open the van's back window and lit up the scene with my ammo, making that bitch look like it was the Fourth of July.

Pow! Pow!

The armored truck officer bust his gun towards us, shattering the back window as Sweetie skidded on the loose gravel down the dark alley.

"Mikey! Mikey!" I called to my partner, who was laid out on the van's floor, suffering from gunshot wounds to his thigh. We hadn't realized he had been hit until after he hopped in the van after snatching two sacks of crispy Benjamin Franklins from the money truck guard earlier when he jumped in the van for our getaway.

"Mikey, answer me!" I yelled again, reloading my gun to aim back at my target.

Pow!

One shot from my rifle to his head and he was instantly executed. I smiled sinisterly as he and his truck fell over the shoulder of the freeway and into the Mississippi River. I felt a great deal of achievement, knowing my big brother would be proud.

I pressed my back against the inside of the van, breathing heavily. I soon snapped back to reality as I looked over at Mikey. I placed my gun to the left of me and crawled over to him.

"Come on, bruh, come on. Answer me, please!" I shook his body as his eyes stared back at me with no motion or life in them. I put two fingers to his neck and checked his pulse. Thank God, he was still breathing.

"Sweetie!" I called to her again as she drove frantically, praying in Spanish for our friend's life. "Get us to the safe house, now! Call Bang and tell him to get Dr. Easy on the way, stat! He's not responding and has already lost too much blood."

"Yes, brother. I'm calling him now, Gwop. Stay up, Mikey, stay up! Don't you close your eyes on us, Papi. Señor, por favor, salve a Mikey. Señor, por favor, salve a Mikey." She cried to Jesus, begging Him to save Mikey's life in her language while she made the phone call to my brother. I pulled our wounded soldier in my arms tightly and rocked, praying for him myself.

Mikey was only nineteen years old. He was too young to lose a life he had yet to begin living. I'd previously told my older brother, Bang, our little partners, Pilla and Mikey, were too young to join our robbery squad, but he didn't give a fuck. The only nigga he gave a damn about was Benjamin Franklin and the other dead presidents.

Even though we were the most anonymous and notorious robbery gang, this shit was starting to get old to me. We were born and raised in the tri-state area, but we had never done a job in or near our hometown of Elizabeth, New Jersey. It was too risky. We'd traveled around the world to many states to fulfill our greed and had never been caught. We never hit the same city or state more than once. The reason why was because we never left a paper trail or any witnesses.

I'd killed many niggas in my profession, but I had a double standard when it came to members of my group, my own family. Honestly, I didn't feel that any amount of money was worth taking a life over.

"We have to switch cars now, Gwop!" Sweetie yelled from the driver's seat as she zoomed into a dimly lit parking garage, breaking the entrance gate on her way in. She parked next to a black Nissan Sentra and hopped out to hotwire it.

I let go of Mikey and leaned back on my knees, opening the back door. I placed both hands on my face and shook my head in distress.

"The car is ready. Come on, Papi," Sweetie said as she pulled Mikey's lifeless legs to help him out the van.

"His eyes closed, ma, he's gone!" I cried as I fell to the ground, staring at his body.

"No, please no!" Her screams echoed through the vacant car parking garage as her medium-brown mascara ran down her pretty face.

My heart was just about to fall out my chest, then I heard his annoying-ass nerdy giggle.

"Nigga, I ain't dead yet," he snickered, easing the aching pain in my heart.

I jumped up from my knees and grabbed him by his shirt. "We gotta get you some help, homie. You bet' not die on me, nigga."

He smiled and nodded while I persuaded him to remain calm while Sweetie got ahold of my brother and our on-call doctor.

♥

I applied pressure to Mikey's wound in the backseat as Sweetie drove like a speed racer to the safe house. As soon as we pulled up, Dr. Easy ran outside and helped me lift our wounded soldier from the backseat and into the garage.

I stood back and watched Dr. Eazy pour vodka into our soldier's wound as he screeched in pain. Doc took his time to remove the bullet from Brains, and by the grace of God, he was successful.

Brains got hit with one bullet in his side, but the doc patched him up and said he would survive with much-needed time off and rest. I wondered where the fuck Bang was. I didn't give a damn how he felt. Tonight, was too fucking risky, and this was my last heist. Period!

♥ Chapter Eleven

BANG

"What, Sweetie? Calm down for me, babe. I can't understand that Spanglish you speaking right now, shorty." I pulled over to the corner of Canal Street.

"It's Mikey, love. He—" I removed my ear from the phone as I scanned my rearview mirror and saw two detectives walking up behind me. I threw my car in drive and sped through the downtown streets of New Orleans as another squad car followed closely on my tail. My adrenaline rose with each turn I made in hopes of fleeing the cop cars that were following closely behind me.

"Fuck!" I screamed as I realized my cell had hit the floor panel. I reached down to retrieve it as my car swerved into oncoming traffic. I darted down a dark alley and decided to do the unthinkable when I saw the cops were no longer that close behind me, but I could hear their sirens approaching my location. I secured my M 11911 .45 Caliber Ghost Gun in my pants, grabbed my phone from the floorboard, and turned off my car lights. I opened my door and jumped out of my moving car, rolling onto the gravel of the dark alley, hiding my body from any potential witnesses. I heard a loud crash and saw that my car had slammed into a city bus and another small vehicle.

Fuck, fuck, fuck! I thought as I jumped to my feet and ran down the alley like Carl Lewis looking for a getaway. Being that I had on all-black during the robbery, I decided to shed some of my clothes to easily blend in with the crowd of drunk partygoers who were partying in the street. I pulled my black hoodie over my head and tossed it inside a makeshift heater some homeless bums nearby had made with an old trashcan. I pulled a stack of money from my pocket and gave both homeless women a crispy hundred-dollar bill.

"See, Bennie, I told you there are still some good people in this crazy world. Let's go down and get us some wine to celebrate. Thanks, Hun." I waved to them and smiled as I turned the corner from the alley to blend in with the crowd and placed my cell to my ear, waiting for my Sweetie to answer.

"Aaron Thompson! Put your hands up! We've got you. It's been a long journey, but now it's time to surrender! Your days of stealing from the government are finished. You're mine now, nigga!" Detective Marissa

Benson shouted in my ear as she pulled my hands down from the air and placed them behind my back to cuff them.

Of all the years my crew had robbed people, we'd always gotten away. I admit I was cocky because we'd never been caught, but this time, we had gotten caught slipping. "Oh, I see you are very excited to see me." She smiled sarcastically as she looked down at my hard dick. I always had an instant erection after a successful getaway. I fucked Sweetie from time to time, but money was what really made me cum.

I sucked my teeth at her as my penis softened. My blood boiled inside. There was no way I would spend one fucking day in prison, and I meant that shit.

♥

My body was cold as it shivered. I could feel water dripping from my head, and I felt as if I was drowning. I tried to shake my head to make the water that filled my ears escape. I attempted to open my heavy eyes, and that was when I realized I must've been hallucinating. I blinked away the blur in my vision until it became clear, and that was when I saw this bitch standing in front of me. I tried to use my hands to wipe the excess water from my face, but that was when I noticed they were cuffed behind the chair I was seated in. When my eyes finally focused, I noticed a tall, slender, black woman dressed in a navy-blue pantsuit was standing in front of me.

"Well, good morning to you, too, Aaron Thompson. How did you sleep?" she snickered sarcastically.

I rolled my eyes and sucked my teeth. This bitch, I thought. "May I ask why the fuck you're harassing me while I'm working?" I was tired of this crazy bitch. I mean, I dicked her down a few times, but I had no intentions of being with her; she was my girl's sister. This bitch thought because she carried a badge and a gun, she was God or something. I got tired of paying her off to keep my secret safe from her sister. This bitch here was a certified stalker. Every single job my crew went on, this hoe was somewhere near, watching a nigga's every move.

"Oh, shut up! You should be glad I'm checking on your ass, nigga. Today was dangerous. I think your crew needs to take a break for a while. The streets are starting to get hot, and y'all are getting a little sloppy since y'all are now one man short—"

I sucked my teeth, shook my head and stopped her words mid-sentence while cutting my eyes at her.

"Oh, I'm so sorry, baby," she said as she dropped down to her knees and tugged at my pants, making my dick rise for the occasion.

"Nah, shorty, I wanna know why you did all this shit. You got me out there in Downtown New Orleans, running for my damn life and shit. Yo, that ain't cool, shorty, for real." Marissa kept my crew and me under the police radar, but everything had a price. I was tired of fucking her dry pussy ass just to keep our secrets safe. Then she was a dog-ass bitch because she was fucking her twin sister's man, and still skinned and grinned in my girl's face daily with remnants of my creamy cum on her breath. It really was a cold world out here. "Yo, where the fuck is my phone? We had an emergency with one of my potnas, and I really need to check on him to see if he is all right, ma, ya know?"

She rolled her eyes and smacked her lips before getting up off her knees and pulling my cell from her back pocket, throwing it into my lap. I gave her a sideways look and rattled the cuffs, letting her know she needed to unlock them so I could use my damn hands. She exhaled and freed my hands, then plopped down on the hotel bed, spreading her long legs like a soaring Eagle, then using her fingers to play with the piercing that peeped out from her freshly waxed kitty cat. I tried hard to keep my composure while I was on the phone, checking on Mikey, but knowing that my crew had just gotten away with another successful robbery had me ready to fuck something to celebrate. Besides, he would live, but I made sure to tell the armor truck driver to wound him for helping Pilla rob me. Sometimes you have to send a warning shot to niggas who played with your fucking money. I couldn't let him die, though; he was a huge asset to my crooked business.

The night the alarm went off at the spot, Marissa had my lookout posted up, watching both men's every move. I didn't know why these niggas tried to play me. I had the law on my side, so anything that happened, I knew about it. Especially when it had to do with anyone in my crew.

♥Chapter Twelve

SHIRI

"So, what's been up with you, BJ? How's everything going at school?" I asked my little brother as he sat across from me in front of the frozen yogurt shop at the mall. We had come out shopping today for our mother's birthday. I knew my mother was a label queen, so our father gave us one of his many credit cards to borrow for the day to get her the perfect gift.

I could tell something was bothering him by the sad look on his face. I brushed my hand across his sandy-brown curly hair to ease his sadness and make him open up a bit.

"I just don't understand why you had to move so far away. I don't like being at home by myself with Mommy all the time, she's boring." I laughed and rose from my seat to embrace him tightly in my arms. My brother and I were very close growing up. I knew he wouldn't take it too well when I decided to leave home, and that was one of the reasons why I'd stayed at my parents' house so long.

"Now, Beej, you know I'm always one FaceTime away." I comforted him, placing my hand on top of his.

"It's just that, I'm an adult now, so I must learn how to live as an adult without the help of our parents. When you become an adult and go to college, you will forget all about your big sister. Especially when you get a girlfriend," I teased him.

"Ewwww, girls are gross!" he gagged, making us both laugh.

We grabbed our shopping bags from the back of the chairs we were sitting in and made our way to the mall's exit.

♥

I looked over at BJ while I switched lanes in one of my father's many foreign cars and smiled. "Now you know you can come visit me in New Jersey anytime. How about this summer? Just me and you, and you can bring your game system to play in my office while I work." I smiled at him.

"That's cool, Ri, but the summer is not coming fast enough. I need a break from Mom and Dad. All they do is argue and fight all the time." I darted my eyes over at him as I used my turning signal to exit the freeway. I was in complete shock about what my brother had revealed to me. My parents and I had close relationships, and I wasn't sure if it was because of the distance that I hadn't noticed, but I had no idea.

"Mommy is cheating on Daddy, that's why they fight all the time!" he shouted and folded his arms across his chest, causing me to slam my foot on the brakes and swerve to avoid hitting a minivan, whose angry driver flipped me the bird and laid on their horn aggressively.

I quickly drove down the street that led to our subdivision and pulled to the side of the street near the small park that was in our neighborhood. My heart crumbled as I heard those words come from his mouth. I knew they hurt him more than me because he now had light tears falling from his eyes. I unbuckled my seatbelt and pulled him into a tight embrace.

"You're far away now, Daddy's always at the office, and Mommy is always with her new boyfriend. When they get a divorce, I'll be left alone while the rest of you go on with your lives," he cried, melting my heart even more. I really hated for my baby brother to feel this way. Deep down, I felt every ounce of BJ's pain, and I really wanted to know more about the situation with my mother, but I knew my mother, and she would never tell me the truth. I had finally started a life on my own in this world, and even though I missed being in Atlanta, I liked the fact that I was far and finally living my life. I didn't want my baby brother to feel like I was neglecting him, and I wasn't sure if he would understand that I was an adult now, who was on my own. But I also didn't want him to feel like he was unloved now that I lived so far away, and my parents were ignoring him to deal with their own secret lives.

♥

I smacked my lips and rolled my eyes before pressing the end button on my cell. This was the fourth time today I'd called Darren, and he hadn't answered. I scrolled through our text message thread and noticed he hadn't responded to any of my messages. I started to get worried. I hoped everything was all right. Him ignoring me had my mind in a whirl. I really wondered if he was laid up with one of those east coast bitches while I was back home visiting. I thought about calling Khodi, so she could call him for me, but decided against it. We weren't in high school anymore.

I did a once-over again in the floor-length mirror in my old room and retouched my lip gloss before grabbing my clutch and heading out the door and down the hallway.

"Shiri!" my mother called from her bedroom. "Can you come in and help me finish getting dressed, please?"

"Coming, Ma!" I made my way to my parents' bedroom, stopping to run my fingers through my baby brother's curly hair as I passed him in the hallway.

"Can you please put your phone games away for Mommy's dinner?" I asked him, playfully snatching his lifeline from him and holding it above my head. He nodded, and I quickly returned it to him.

As I walked into my parents' room, my stomach twisted up in knots. I walked up behind my mother, who was seated at her vanity, applying Mary Kay foundation to her face.

"You called me, Ma?" I forced out a smile. I wiped my sweaty palms on the side of my dress slacks before gently placing them on her broad shoulders. "You look so beautiful, Mommy," I complimented as our eyes connected in the mirror.

My whole life, I had looked up to my mother. She was my everything. I was always taught to carry myself as a lady, and whenever I married my husband, to be his one and only and to be by his side through thick and thin. The conversation I had earlier with BJ kept replaying in my mind. It hurt my heart to learn of the secret truth my parents were hiding from us.

"Ri, baby, hook this up for me, please?" she asked while holding one of her many diamond encrusted necklaces on her chest. I did as she asked, trying hard to hold back the many questions I wanted to ask about her side piece. It was always the judgmental ones who hid the deepest secrets.

"Anything else you need me to help you with, Ma?" She tapped my hand and shook her head no, and I prepared to exit and meet my brother and father downstairs.

"Mmm-hmm." She smacked her lips and shook her head while glimpsing at the news that was playing on the sixty-five-inch TV screen that hung on her and my father's wall. "Damn thugs always wanna take away from hard working people out here in the world." I stopped in my tracks and walked to the loveseat that sat at the foot of my parents' California king-sized canopy bed and watched the screen. As the news reporter spoke, I sat in a daze and stared at the gunman's tattoo. I shook my head and closed my eyes tightly, swallowing the lump in my throat, being sure to hide my expressions from my judgmental mother.

"Earlier today at a local Super Walmart in Kenner, Louisiana, an armored truck was robbed. Police are saying this could've been an inside job. As of now, we currently have a count of two fatalities; police have not released the names of the victims…"

I stared at the picture of the familiar tattoo on the arm that was extended out the back window, aiming at the armored truck. I couldn't believe my eyes. The man I was madly in love with was a thief and a killer. This couldn't be my life right now. I pulled my cell out my clutch and scrolled my call log again to see that I had no missed calls from Darren.

"Ri!" my mother called, snapping me out of my trance. "Are you ready, baby? Let's head out."

"Yes, ma'am," I responded and nodded, following her lead downstairs.

On the way to my mother's birthday dinner, I was completely silent. My heart burned with pain, and my mind was full of confusion. After all the moments we'd shared with each other. Now I knew why he could always afford to take me on expensive dates. No telling what else he was hiding from me.

I took a handkerchief and batted the corners of my eyes to pat the tears from my eyes as my father pulled up to Perry's steakhouse.

During my mother's birthday dinner, my mind kept traveling back to the king cobra snake tattoo that was wrapped around the suspect's forearm as he fired gunshots from the back of the getaway van shown. I poked at the prime rib that sat in front of me as my mind traveled back to the day, I'd met Darren in the bodega.

He was dressed in designer labels from head to toe, and the icy watch he rocked on his wrist cost more than what I made each month. At first, I thought maybe he was a street nigga. Even that was something I could've swallowed easier than a bank robber. When we went out on dates, he asked me all types of questions about my job, and now I thought he wasn't that into me, but just wanted to know about where I worked so he could stick up the place. Part of me wanted to cut his bitch ass for leading me on, and the other part of me wanted to fuck the shit out of him. Knowing that he lived this secret, savage life turned me on inside. I was more than ready to get back to Jersey to find out exactly what was going on with this man I had fallen deeply in love with.

"Ri, is everything OK, honey bun?" my father Brandon asked, pulling me from my thoughts, and quickly bringing me back to reality.

"Yes, daddy, I'm fine. I'll be back." I stood and kissed him on the cheek as I excused myself to the ladies' room. I dialed Darren's line again and was sent to his voicemail after only one ring. As I walked down the dimly lit hallway that led to the restrooms, I accidentally bumped into a couple who stood there, swallowing each other's tongues while their hands groped their body parts as if they were the only ones in the building. When the man turned and faced me, his brown skin turned ghost white as it revealed he was my best friend Khodi's father. But the woman who stood behind him held her head down in shame. She should've been embarrassed because it was my mother.

I rolled my eyes at the two of them before I turned away and stormed off, back to the dinner table. I could hear my mother calling my name, but I decided not to turn around. If I had, I probably would have slapped the shit out of her hoe ass for disrespecting my father like he wasn't sitting at the table just a few feet away.

Tears streamed down my face as I screamed for my father, alarming the other guests in the expensive restaurant. "Daddy! I want to go, now!"

"Baby, what's wrong?" My father wrapped me in his strong arms and dried my tears with his handkerchief.

"I want to go back home, now," I said through gritted teeth as I looked back at my mother, who was slowly walking towards our table as her side piece dipped off, so my father couldn't see him. From this day forth, I would no longer have any respect for my mother. She was a prime example of bitches I hated. Hoes who walked around like they were better than everyone were the ones who had the biggest secrets. Right now, I didn't care what Darren did; I would rather be laid up in his arms than witnessing just how much of a slut my mother was.

The hostess came to our table to see if everything was fine, and I grabbed my shawl and clutch from my seat and sped walked out of the restaurant. When I made it to the parking lot, my younger brother was on my trail. He stood beside me, speechless. I pulled him into my arms, causing more tears to fall from my weeping eyes. "You were right, BJ. I just witnessed our mother and her boyfriend making out like teenagers in the restroom hallway."

We broke our embrace and turned to our father, who walked up behind us.

"Baby girl, what's wrong?"

"What's wrong? Our mother, your wife, was by the ladies' room with her tongue down your best friend's and business partner's throat!"

He stood in confusion and turned around to face our mother who stood behind him.

"So, this shit between you two is still going on?"

"Wait a minute, Daddy, you knew?" He put his head down in shame as I backed away from him as he tried to grab me to comfort me. Everyone I loved in my life was feeding me lies, and at this moment, I just wanted to be alone. I pulled up my Uber app and saw that one was near me. I quickly requested a pickup, and within minutes, the driver pulled up to take me away from the shocking truths my family had just revealed.

♥

My parents' home was about forty-five minutes from the restaurant, and that gave me plenty of time to think about all the craziness that was going on in my life. I decided that instead of staying the extra day I intended, I would leave that night and catch an earlier flight. I couldn't spend another night in a home that was filled with lies. When my driver pulled up to the home, I asked him to wait while I went inside to pack my belongings. On the way downstairs, my parents and brother walked inside.

"Ri, please don't go. Please! I'll miss you!" BJ screamed.

As bad as I didn't want to hurt my brother, I had to leave. I was now an adult and had my own life to live. I loved my parents dearly, but I could no longer respect the fact that my mother was a lying, cheating whore, and my father was OK with her decision to be just that. Then, to add insult to injury, it was Khodi's father, someone I'd grown to know and love as an uncle. I felt so disrespected and embarrassed, I had no choice but to leave. I removed my parents' house key from my key ring, sat it on the table in the foyer and turned to BJ. "I'm so sorry. I'll love you forever, and you can always come visit, but my life isn't here anymore. I love you, Beej." I kissed him on his cheek and gave him a hug before rolling my suitcase out the door, planning to never return again.

Chapter Thirteen

SHIRI

My little brother blew my phone up from the time I walked out of my parents' house until I reached the airport. I didn't want to hurt him by leaving the way I had, but it was best. At that moment, my heart was hurting, and just about everyone I loved was hiding major secrets from me.

I took an Uber from the airport to my condo. I was glad I still had two days off until I was scheduled to return to work. After the news I found out from my parents and Darren, I needed to be alone for a little while. I rode the elevator up to my floor and slowly walked to my apartment door with my head down. When I heard the locks from Khodi's apartment being unlocked across the hallway, I hurriedly snatched my door open and ran inside, locking my door. I could hear her talking to a man with a deep baritone voice, so I stood on my tippy toes, looking through my peephole to see who it was. I identified the man as her boo, Kendrick. He looked as if he was disturbed by something, and the way they ran to the elevator, let me know it had to be some sort of emergency.

♥

Me: I'm back home now. Are you still coming by?

After unpacking and getting myself situated, I texted Darren to see if he still wanted to talk. Even though I was mad at him, at this moment, being wrapped up in his muscular, chocolate arms would cure my aching heart.

Sneaky Ass Nigga: Yeah Shorty. I'll be there in about thirty minutes.

I exhaled deeply and walked to open my front door for Khodi. She called me and said she needed to talk to me about something important.

"Hey, boo, what's up? Wait, what's wrong, Ri?" My best friend pulled me by the arms and led me to the sofa. I tried to hide the way I felt from all the recent pain I'd experienced over the weekend at my parents', but the pain I tried hard to bury seeped from my eyes as soon as I saw Khodi's face.

"Nothing, girl, just allergies," I lied. "What's up with you, though?"

"Well, girl, I know you've seen on the news about the notorious gang that's been hitting all across the country, right?" I nodded, trying hard to hold my tongue from revealing our parents' secret. "Girl, well, Kendrick is, well, was a part of that crew. Do you know that last night, we were getting ready to take a shower, and when I went to get his ringing cell from his book bag, I found—"

"Did you know that my mother and your father have been having an affair!" I blurted out.

She looked at me with wide eyes and nodded, then lowered her head. "Wait! You knew, Khodisha? And you didn't say shit to me about it—"

"Ri, everyone knows." She cut me off, staring at me with a smirk on her face. "The two of them have been fucking each other since we were kids." She laughed nonchalantly.

I looked down at an incoming text message from Darren. "Khodi, I need some time alone right now. Can you leave? I'll talk to you later."

She agreed and left my apartment. I read over the message from Darren over and over again, praying my eyes were not playing tricks on me. I couldn't believe I had opened my heart up to this lying-ass nigga.

GWOP

Me: Look, I'm sorry shorty, but some real fucked up shit happened to one of my li'l potnas. I've been trying to make sure he's good and check on my grandfather. I can come by later boo, just trust me, please.

Southern Booty: OK Darren, whatever.

I hadn't spoken to Shiri in almost a week, and I knew I had fucked up with her. After all this shit that happened with the last job, I just wanted to run far away from everybody.

I walked into the meeting room and sat down at the table with an uneasiness in my stomach. Dr. Easy said that Mikey was doing better since the day he was shot, but he still wasn't able to walk without assistance. He still had a few more weeks to heal before he could do so. I looked around the room, viewing the empty chairs that were placed around the table that were usually filled with members of our crew. Since the Cali job, Pilla had been M.I.A., Brains was injured, and the Doc had just walked in with an agitated look on his face.

"What's up, Doc?" I greeted and stood to dap him up.

Sweetie walked in and spoke to us before taking her seat. Silence was very unusual for her, and she wasn't dolled up with her expensive MAC makeup and vibrant acrylic nails as she usually would be. I could tell from the tension between the two of them that some shit was about to go bad.

I checked my phone as an incoming text came in from Bang.

"Bang just hit me and said he'll be pulling up in about twenty minutes."

Sweetie crossed her arms over her chest and nodded, and the Doc shook his head.

"Aye, what's going on, Son? Is it some shit I need to know about?" I laughed. "Both of your facial expressions are telling me y'all know some shit I must not know. What up, what got you bugging the fuck out?"

"Papi, I'm just here to get my cut, and I'm gone," Sweetie said to me, not looking my way.

"Yeah, this will probably be my last job with you guys. I didn't sign up for this secretive shit. And to find out that Brains was an intended target—"

"Wait? What! Who the fuck said that shit?"

Sweetie connected eyes with Doc that let me know she confirmed the statement he'd made, then sat back in her chair and looked my way.

"Aye, just tell him to Cash App me my shit. I'm gone!" Dr. Easy stormed out of the meeting room with no remorse.

"Sweetie, what's going on? Just talk to me, ma. Who said this shit about Brains being a fucking target?"

She looked me in my eyes, and hers welled up with tears. "The streets been talking, Papi. Some shit about that bitch Benson, the detective. The driver you murked was working for her. The whole thing about the truck being fifteen minutes late that day was a planned stunt and Pilla said that he—" She stopped mid-sentence and quickly focused her eyes on something behind me, and that was when I felt my brother's presence in the meeting room.

"Is there something you need to talk to me about, little brother?" Bang's voice boomed from behind me.

I turned around, full of anger, and stepped to his face. "Yo, you need to leave that fucking magic dust alone, nigga, because it got you bugging the fuck out! Brains, though, nigga? Of all niggas! And he's the one who does damn near everything for our crew. You fucking foul. I don't know what's gotten into you lately, but you wilding, dawg!" I yelled, pointing my finger in his face as he stood in front of me, grinning like a sly fox with no worries in the world.

"I ain't doing the next job. I'm done with this shit!" I left the meeting room and jogged to my whip. My heart burned with hate for my only flesh and blood. I couldn't believe my brother would stoop this low and harm a member of our crew. This shit wasn't right. I was so fucking pissed off, I accidentally ran through a red light, almost causing a head-on collision with a large truck. I zoomed all the way to Shiri's condo because, at this moment, she was the only thing in this world that could give me peace.

♥

As I rode the elevator up to her floor, my stomach twisted up in knots. During all of our successful heists, no person in our crew had ever been injured. Even though we knew what the risks were for our lifestyle, we felt it was a major blessing that no man had ever been hurt. When I got to Shiri's floor and exited the elevator, I scrolled to her name to let her know I had arrived. The doorman had gotten used to me, so the last couple of times I'd visited, he would let me up without buzzing her first. I usually came with some expensive gift tucked under my arms for my new lady.

As I walked down her hallway, I noticed a familiar person walking my way. I noticed it was Pilla, and he gave me a head nod before passing me up and stepping into the elevator.

"Aye, hold the door!" I yelled at him, turning around and joining him to get more information on Mikey's injury. I cleared my call screen and decided to send Shiri a text instead.

Me: Look, I'm so sorry shorty, but I got a lot going on with my family right now. I'll get at you when I can, but tonight or probably any time soon isn't a good time. Again, I'm sorry I couldn't make it.

♥ Chapter Fourteen

BANG

"Yeah, fuck you, too, bruh!" I shouted before I hung up with Gwop.

I didn't know much about the little bitch he had been fucking lately, but she really had that nigga's head far up in the damn clouds. I rolled my eyes as I pulled in front of me and Rissa's place. I opened my glove box and pulled out a small pack of my magic dust. Cocaine was one hell of a drug, and when I had it in my system, I felt invincible.

I had been snorting this shit since my teenage years, and even though I promised Karissa I would stop doing drugs, I had to be full of something to deal with her nagging on a daily. I scooped a small amount of the addictive drug up with my car key and inhaled the stimulant through my right nostril quickly. My throat expanded, and my tongue numbed a bit, but the way my body immediately felt as if I were floating on a mountain of clouds kept me calm.

I hopped out my whip and jogged around to the sidewalk that led to our house and ran up the small steps that were on the stoop. As I walked in the door, Rissa was in the hallway, kneeling over Pop-Pop. I ran over to them and dropped to my knees to see what was going on.

"Aaron—" His words struggled from his lips. "Come on, Pop, not now. Please don't leave me. If you leave me, I'll kill you. Please stay with me until the medics get here," I begged him. I didn't know what I would do without my grandfather anymore. Within ten minutes, the foyer of our home was filled with EMTs who attached wires and tubes to my grandfather's body.

"Ris, call the paramedics and see if your sister can stay here with you. I'll follow them to the ER." I looked over at my grandfather as weakness filled his body. Over the past couple of years, Pop-Pop had had two strokes, and at this moment, he was clutching his chest as if he was having a heart attack. It would hurt me to the core if he lost his life right now. He and my brother were all I had left of my parents.

♥

The whole ride to the hospital, I rode in silence as I followed the ambulance closely. I called my brother's line, and he sent me to voicemail twice. I could've texted him, but I felt that if he really wanted to know what the emergency was, he would pick up the phone or call me back. My brother and I were thick as thieves growing up.

After the death of our parents traumatized me at such an early age, I hated every single government official who crossed my path. I'd always had a problem with authority, and every single time this bitch came around, she irked my fucking guts. I rolled my eyes and angrily blew air from my lips when Karissa wobbled through the emergency room doors with her worrisome-ass sister following her. I was tired of dealing with this bitch, and I was definitely tired of paying her off with my hard-earned money and dick.

"Mami, didn't I tell you to stay at the house? You big and pregnant, you don't need to be up here on your feet,

Ris." I chastised my baby mama, completely ignoring the presence of her annoying-ass sister.

"They took him to the back and are running some tests on him. They think he had a slight heart attack, so as soon as they admit him into a room, we can see him. I gotta go take a leak."

I kissed Karissa on the cheek and excused myself to the men's room while her sister stood with her arms folded across her chest. After relieving myself, I washed my hands and checked my phone to see if my brother had hit me back. As soon as I stepped foot out of the men's room, Marissa was in my face.

"Hey, brother-in-law, or should I say, Big Zaddy?" she teased me and bit her lower lip while grabbing a handful of my dick. I smirked at her and slapped it away with the quickness.

"Yo, you fucking buggin', for real. And where is Ris?"

"She's in the back with Pop-Pop. They finally gave him a room."

"OK, so why the fuck you out here jockin' a nigga when I'm tryna take a piss?" I stared her worrisome ass up and down as she stood there, looking dumbfounded. I knew I was wrong for fucking my main bitch's identical twin sister, but it kind of just happened. Like, it wasn't planned, but I had to do something to shut this bitch up about my gig. If word got out that my crew was the one that had the FBI running around, chasing their tails, my whole empire would crumble, and I wasn't going to let that happen, so I played the cards that were dealt to me.

I brushed past Marissa, walking to the nurses' station to find out what hall they had put Pop-Pop in when she stopped me.

"All bullshit to the side, Bang, I need to talk to you about some serious shit." I stopped in my tracks and quickly turned back to this needy bitch with my eyebrows turned up in agitation.

"Let's step outside, so I can have a quick smoke," I told her, removing a pack of Camels from my jean pocket. She nodded and followed me to the smoking area. I looked down at my phone to see the time before lighting the tip of my cancer stick. I inhaled the refreshing, strong tobacco and blew it from my lips, giving her a look that let her know she needed to hurry the fuck up with whatever she had to tell me so I could get back inside and away from her always-begging-for-dick ass.

"So, I'm just going to be honest with you. I don't think y'all should go through with the last job at Tri-State."

"What do you mean, we shouldn't do it?" I asked, getting agitated by her presence. I swear the only time I could deal with this dumb bitch was if she was bent over, tooting her fat ass on my dick or kneeling in between my legs, swallowing my stiff rod. She nagged just like her damn sister.

"It's just that, I feel it's too risky. It's too close to home, and I don't want anything bad to happen—"

I put my hand up to stop her while clearing my lungs, blowing out the last of my smoke and ashing my cigarette before tossing it over the balcony.

"Don't you think it's time to wrap this lifestyle up? You will be a father soon, and my nephews need a man at home who's living a legit life, not in the streets, robbing, killing people, and coming up off of free money!"

I wrapped my hands so tight around that bitch's neck, I was seconds away from snapping it in two. The audacity of this bitch. I couldn't fault anyone but myself for fucking with her fraud ass. I snapped back into reality and let go of Marissa as she struggled to catch her breath. "How could you do this to me? You put your hands on me after I put my life and job on the line for your ass, nigga? Really? I lied and killed for you, and if I didn't love my pregnant sister, I wouldn't have done anything."

"Yo' ass got a lot to say, even though you still fucking your twin sister's man!" I shouted, drawing attention from the Robocop security guard who was making his rounds. I nodded to him to let him know everything was OK before gritting my teeth at Marissa's hoe ass and turning from where she stood to make my way back into the hospital.

"You know what, I should tell Ris everything! Even what you did to our parents!" she shouted. I turned to that bitch once more and gave her an evil look, then shot that hoe the finger and walked inside the double doors of the hospital to check on my grandfather.

After getting Pop-Pop's room information from the nurse at the front, I walked down the hallway to the elevators to go to his floor. I hated that blackmailing bitch. I was close to getting somebody to off her ass. This hoe knew too many of my secrets and used them against me every single time. Honestly, I hated that my girl was pregnant because I wanted nothing to do with either one of them anymore. As I rode up to the fifth floor on the elevator, thoughts ran through my head from the night this crazy bitch mentioned earlier.

Two nights after our parents were murdered on national TV, I heard my grandfather arguing with Uncle Rob in the hallway.

"Tell me the truth, Robbie, or I'ma blow ya fucking brains all over the floor. I'ma ask you once more before I do so. Now, I just left the pool hall, and Johnny's boys put a bug in my ear that you had something to do with Connie and Chrissy's murder! Answer me, fucker!" Pop-Pop screamed, spitting into Uncle Rob's face as he grabbed his collar. Robbie laughed in his face, then pushed Pop-Pop out his face with all his might, causing Pop-Pop's gun to hit the floor, firing a bullet through the wall of the Williams' apartment and piercing Mrs. Williams' heart. As the men went round for round, I watched and scooped up my grandfather's gun. I stood there with sweaty palms and shaky hands.

"That's right, I gave the cops the heads up on the Cali job. Chrissy's bitch ass shouldn't have been holding out on me. I found the stash from the last job. Karma caught up with him and his bitch!" He laughed as he tried to block Pop-Pop's jabs. My grandfather was an older man, but he could still fight like Muhammad Ali.

Hearing those words from the man I trusted, I fired two fatal rounds into the skull of Robert Williams, causing his instant death. His heavy body fell hard on the wooden floor, almost breaking it. I shot him again in the back and walked into the Williams' apartment to fire three more rounds into his wife. I looked over at their young twin daughters who were only four years old at the time.

Pop-Pop grabbed the twins and my brother Darren and strapped them in their car seats while he and I drenched their deceased bodies in gasoline. I did the honor of lighting the match that burned them and our home into ashes. When we returned to the car, I noticed Marissa had been watching us the entire time. She'd always been a nosy bitch. Our grandfather told the police he had taken us all out for ice cream the night we killed the Williamses.

We drove to the river, and I watched Pop-Pop throw the gun away I had used to murder the sorry motherfuckers who had caused my parents' death. From this day forth, I would hate the law forever.

So, I hated this Marissa bitch. She knew things about me that not even my brother knew. He always wondered why our grandfather had nicknamed me Bang. It was because I had committed my first murder at such a young age.

Two Weeks Later

♥Chapter Fifteen

GWOP

I dialed my brother's line again for the third time, and it went to voicemail.

Fuck! I thought. This nigga had really been tripping out lately.

Ring! Ring!

I exhaled, and my nervousness eased as an incoming call came to my phone from my brother's line.

"Yo, what's up?" I answered with my left hand while I steered my whip with my right.

"Gwop? Hey, it's me, Papi," Sweetie started with a shaky voice. "I need you to come meet me now, please. It's Bang. He's full of that powder and tripping!"

"Ay, where are y'all? Put him on the phone, ma," I told her as I switched lanes to exit the freeway.

"Aaron, Aaron, come here, baby. Your brother is on the line. Talk to him for me, please, Papi!" she begged. I could hear my irate brother yelling vulgarly, followed by screams from Sweetie. I knew he was probably high off his favorite drug, cocaine, and he didn't want to hear shit I had to say, but I had to try to get to him.

"What the fuck you want, bruh? You ain't been checking on your blood since you been fucking your new li'l pussy, so tell me why you calling now?" He breathed heavily into the phone.

"Yo, you tripping, man. For real, where are you? Let's meet up and lemme holla at you, dawg," I persuaded him.

"Ain't shit to talk about anymore! Ma and Pa gone, neither one of my bitches ain't shit, and the kids probably ain't mine either, son! Pop-Pop gone, too, so what am I supposed to do now? You were all I had left, and you chose a piece of southern pussy over your only flesh and blood!" He screamed into the phone as tears distorted his voice, and that stung my heart.

"Big bro, no one could ever come between us. You know that. Just tell me where you are, and I'll come get you so we can talk this out, brother," I pleaded, frantically speeding down the street, avoiding traffic signals and taking back streets to get to the spot before my brother hurt himself or anyone else.

I heard him crank his ignition. "It's too late. You know that last job we were 'posed to pull at your bitch's bank? Well, I'll tell her you said hello. I'm pulling up now." He let out a sinister laugh before disconnecting our phone call. I redialed his number three times, and he sent me to voicemail with each call. I pulled over on the feeder road to calm my anxiety and gather my thoughts. I dialed Shiri's line, praying she answered my call. She hadn't spoken to me in almost two weeks after finding out my secrets, but I couldn't fault her for being upset with me. I'd never in my life felt this way about a woman, and it was killing me to know she wanted nothing more to do with me. I loved shorty and was going to do anything I had to keep her out of harm's way. Even if that meant going against the grain, my only living relative, and big brother.

I did a U-turn and hopped back on the freeway, heading east to Tri-State Financial. I continued to call both my brother and Shiri's phones as I whipped down the freeway, panicking. I didn't know exactly what I could do, but I needed to get her out of that bank, ASAP!

Southern Booty: What do you want nigga? Look, I'm not into guys who have secret lives. Please just leave me alone.

Me: I need you to answer me, please? Isn't it almost lunch time? Can you meet me at that bodega we first met?

Southern Booty: I have a client that just walked in, I'll talk to you later Darren.

I skidded onto the feeder road, almost getting side swiped by an 18-wheeler that was hauling fuel. I made it to Main Street and let out a sigh of relief, until I was quickly halted by the police officers who stood outside, directing traffic. I had forgotten today was the Juneteenth celebration parade, so there was no way I could make it down the street to the bank before my brother arrived to carry out his mission. I angrily turned around and sped down the side street, avoiding traffic signals and pedestrians. I double parked my Jag in the middle of the street and hopped out. I ran down the long alley, looking for a shortcut to get to my baby as quickly as I could. My cell rang in my pocket, and

I pulled it out with the quickness, seeing that it was Shiri calling.

I stopped in my tracks and placed my phone on my ear as my heart beat rapidly, almost out of my chest.

"Hey, Mami. Did you change your mind—" I was instantly cut off when I heard heavy breathing from my brother's voice flow through the phone.

"Sorry, brother. It's me." He let out a wicked laugh. "And to think, I just knew you would've made it here before I did. Now, I'm going to pass the phone to your bitch. Tell her to open the fucking safe for me, or it's lights out for her," he threatened.

"Fuccckk!" I screamed, making a group of pigeons flock away. As I walked closer to the bank, I heard the sirens of the squad cars approaching. "Think about what you're doing! Come on, it's not worth your freedom, man!" I screamed, praying to get through his stubbornness. "Just leave, bro. Leave now and avoid the pigs like we have with every other job. Come on, you don't have to do this. I'm coming around to the front to get you. Leave before they come. They're close, I can hear 'em!" I shouted.

I tried to run to the front of the building to get a better view of the commotion that was taking place, but with the nosy pedestrians, and the on-going parade and traffic, it was impossible. Before I made it to the tall glass doors of the bank, the police had stopped the parade and had the building surrounded. They hopped out their cars with guns drawn, and it was then I knew today would probably be the last day of my brother's life if he didn't surrender to them or me. I ran across the street to Jimmy's bodega where I first met the love of my life and tried to blend in with the crowd of onlookers while my phone stayed glued to my ear.

"How dare you do this, Darren!" I heard Shiri scream in the background. "So, this whole time, I was nothing but another one of your targets? How could you?!" she yelled again, breaking my heart.

I felt like today was going to be the end of our notorious heists, and possibly my brother's life. I heard gunshots echoing in the background as people screamed. I looked through the window of the bodega and saw the news reporter standing in front of the bank, letting the world know what was taking place. Instantly, my mind drifted back to the day I witnessed my parents murdered in cold blood by the police. No matter how hard I tried, I had to eventually face the fact that my brother had just set up his own suicide mission.

"This is Donna Hughes, reporting live from Tri-State Financial downtown. Police have the building surrounded as a hostage situation is now taking place inside. Police say they are not sure of the exact numbers of hostages and victims, but shots were fired, and a negotiator is now on the scene to see if we can come to an agreeance with the suspect who has been identified as Aaron Thompson.

Thompson has finally been identified by witnesses standing by as the leader of the most notorious robbery gang. This gang has hit many places over the past few years and has never been caught by police. But today, the many heists this crew has escaped has come to an end. We are not sure if the suspect is working alone or with a crew…"

I rolled my eyes as the news anchor continued. I looked down at my phone and saw the line had been disconnected. I continued walking closer to the bank, and that was when I heard the watching crowd gasp in awe. The front doors of the bank opened, and several men and women dressed in casual clothing, who I assumed were employees of Tri-State Financial, walked out with their hands in surrender mode. I exhaled softly and nodded, silently praying that my brother and my shorty were coming out unharmed.

Just then, I saw her face. Shiri walked to the door with her hands surrendered and beads of sweat dripping from her forehead. Before she could get one foot out the door, Bang grabbed her in a headlock and pulled her back inside, placing his gun to her right temple as she trembled, and her eyes grew wide.

I brushed my hands down my face and shook my head. I loved my brother with all my heart, but the shit he was doing was really fucked up. I wish he'd left those fucking drugs alone because they had turned him into a monster. With all the spots we'd hit, I knew for a fact this nigga was good on money. I felt he had an obsession with robbing people with the way his adrenaline rose, and his eyes bulged out of his head. His mouth even watered during meetings when we planned our cases, but then again, it could've been from his best friend, Mr. Booga Sugar. He couldn't live without it.

This time, he had gone too far. We had already lost our parents, and now Pop Pop was dead and gone. I had to face it; my brother had officially lost his mind. This nigga had really gone psycho overnight.

The cops surrounded the entrance of the bank and gave their last orders for my brother to surrender himself and his last hostage. Moments later, the door opened, and Shiri frantically ran as fast as she could. The paramedics who were on standby quickly swaddled her in a large rescue blanket. I stared at her with a hurt heart and trembling hands. Her eyes connected with mine and she gave me the deadliest stare, crushing my heart even more.

I hated myself more than anything at this moment. I never wanted things to escalate this far between us. I'd shown her parts of me that no one else had ever seen before. I didn't know how I would be able to live without her, but I was going to do whatever I had to do to get mami back.

Moments later, my brother stumbled from the entrance doors with an AR-15 rifle in his hands. Immediately, two officers ran to him, trying to disarm him. Gunshots rang out as bullets from Bang's weapon pierced the men's chests, causing them to drop to the warm concrete to their deaths. The rest of the team wasted no time emptying their clips into my brother.

I watched in painful awe as his soul left his body permanently. I knew from this moment on, I was alone in this cruel world. Every single person I'd ever loved, I'd lost in a matter of twenty-four hours.

The police attempted to clear the crowd as I stood there, completely still. I watched them cover my brother's body with a white sheet as he laid dead, in cold blood, as my parents had so many years ago. They had him lying there for almost twelve hours, and I didn't move from where I stood until they placed his chilled body in a black body bag and threw him into the coroner's van.

I knew my brother had serious issues, but I wish I could've stopped him before it went this far.

♥Chapter Sixteen

Three Weeks Later…

SHIRI

I felt defeated. I finally had a chance at this thing called adulthood, and I had failed already. I was ashamed and embarrassed that I had to go back home with my parents. I knew they would be arriving in less than two hours to drag me back home, down south where I would never get another chance to face the world on my own. I had lost a career I loved, my best friend, the first man I was ever in love with, and my mind. Maybe being back home was best. I wouldn't be anything more than an Atlanta housewife who lived off my husband as my mother did.

I went to my closet, grabbed my suitcases and made sure I had everything before calling the doorman from downstairs to help me load my things. I wanted so badly to walk over to Khodi's place to talk to her, but I decided against it. I heard three light knocks on my apartment door and wondered who it could be. In this building, no visitors were allowed up without the tenants' permission. I checked my camera, and my mouth dropped when I saw the top of his dread-filled head as he looked down. I exhaled deeply before unhooking the chain latch on the door and snatching it open.

He scooped me into his arms and placed soft kisses down my neck while carrying me to my bedroom. He softly placed me on my bed, pulled apart my legs, and laid in between them.

"Ri, I'm so sorry, shorty. Look at me, I'm sorry. You are the greatest woman I've ever met, and I'm sorry I didn't tell you the truth about me from the beginning, but I didn't want to hurt you, baby. I—"

I placed my finger on his lips so he would stop speaking. At this moment, I didn't care about his past. I just wanted to secure a future with him. I loved this man with all my heart, and I was ready and willing to explore life with him from this day forth. He was my everything, as I was his. He might have pulled off many heists, but who knew that the first day I met him at that bodega downtown, he would steal my heart. If I had to be the Bonnie to his

Clyde, I was down with that. I deserved him, and he deserved me.

I made love to my man for the next couple of hours. We showered, then I grabbed my suitcases and headed out the door with him, hand in hand, smiling. When we approached the elevator, the doors opened, revealing my parents and younger brother, and I instantly came back to reality from the cloud of love I was floating on.

"Shiri Marks, where are you going, baby doll, and who is this gentleman?" my mother asked with her nose turned up, looking Darren up and down.

My man tried letting go of my hand, but I squeezed his tightly to stop him. "Mommy, Daddy, this is my man, Gw—Darren Thompson. We are in love, and we are leaving for Vegas to elope!" I shrieked, pissing my mother off even more.

I placed a kiss on my brother's cheek, pulled my man onto the elevator, and waved goodbye to my parents, who stood in shock.

"I'm sure you want to share this special moment with someone you love, right, bae?" my man whispered in my ear as the elevator stopped on the first floor and the doors opened. Standing in the lobby, waiting for us, was my best friend, Khodi, and her man, Pilla. A wide smile spread across my face as I ran into her open arms.

"I love you so much, best friend!" I reminded her as I squeezed her tightly in my embrace. Our men grabbed our bags, and we walked outside and jumped into my soon-to-be husband's drop-top El Camino.

I slid my Gucci sunglasses on my face, turned to my man, and swallowed his lips.

"So, where are we going when we leave Vegas?" My man smiled as he intertwined our fingers and hit the highway.

"Well, I think we should move to Cali and open up our very own bank!" He lifted my hand to his lips, placed a soft kiss on it and nodded.

"It's whatever you want to do, mami." He smiled before concentrating back on the road.

"Whoop, whoop! We're going to California, baby!" Khodi shouted and embraced me from behind. I turned up the dial on the radio as "Him and I" by G-Eazy & Halsey played through the car stereo.

THE END!

Thanks for Reading!

Authoress Ms. Grad Marie's Catalog

Share my World with a Savage Like You 1&2
**Complete Series

Stealing the Heart of a Dirty South Hustla' 1-3
**Complete Series

Ash & Omar Forever Loving A Dirty South Hustla', (Spin-off to Stealing the Heart of a Dirty South Hustla' Series)

Diary of a Single Mother, Standalone Novel

Love Heist: He robbed my heart, Novella

A Thin Line Between Baby Mama And B*tch! 1&2 Complete Series

Hooked on a Fifth Ward Menace 1&2** Complete Series

She Fell in love with a Southside Dopeboy, 1&2

When a Gangsta Falls for a Real One, *Standalone novel

Caught up in the Wrath of a Hitta's Love, Episode 1&2

Thankful for my Lil Thug, Novella

Christmas with the Smith's, Holiday Novella

All titles FREE with Kindle Unlimited
subscription!!

https://amzn.to/2Br9g95